SUICIDE OR DEATH

A TANNER NOVEL - BOOK 7

REMINGTON KANE

INTRODUCTION

SUICIDE OR DEATH – A TANNER NOVEL – BOOK 7

Sara Blake offers Tanner a no-win proposition.

ACKNOWLEDGMENTS

I write for you.

—Remington Kane

QUOTE

"Do I not destroy my enemies when I make them my friends?"
—Abraham Lincoln

1
A MAN WITH A PLAN

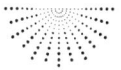

Tanner could feel the stitches in his side strain against the wounded flesh they held together, but he ignored the pain and just kept working on the bolts.

He was in the basement of a restaurant that had been closed for many years. He'd been taken there after surrendering to Sara Blake, to save the life of Laurel Ivy.

After wallowing in unaccustomed melancholy and despair for a time, Tanner went to work doing what he did best and thought up a way to kill his captor, namely, Sara Blake.

He wasn't in a room but was on the inside of a huge walk-in freezer that still retained the faint scent of raw meat, although, he would guess that none had been stored there for years.

There was a long metal table just feet from him that was attached to the opposite wall of the freezer. Someone had welded wrist and ankle restraints at its corners, which could be swung closed on hinges and secured with padlocks.

Beneath the table was a drain that was already stained

red from the years of butchered meat that had dripped blood, and it would act as a drain for human blood if so needed.

Despite Sara's earlier assertion that she wouldn't torture him, Tanner still didn't like the look of that table and had spent hours trying to ignore it, while working on a plan of escape.

He had come up empty.

The handcuffs he had been wearing were connected to a chain that ran down from the ceiling and they had been no problem, not once he managed to maneuver his hands from behind his back.

Sara Blake's lackey, a man named Duke, had checked him over for weapons but had failed to find the handcuff key he had hidden on his person. The key was part of the shoelaces of his boots. It sat at the tip of the lace and was hidden by a black rubber cap.

The laces had been acquired from a spy shop on the internet, had cost him fifteen dollars, and Tanner considered it some of the best money he had ever spent.

Once his hands were free, he went to work on the leg irons, but found that the handcuff key was useless in opening them.

Still, with the cuffs off, he was free of the chain and could move around, although, due to the leg irons, his movement was restricted to a hesitant shuffling gait. He had made his way to the door to see if he could breach it.

It was useless.

The door was thick, made of metal, and he had seen on his way inside the freezer that there were two iron bars slid across its width to keep it from opening.

He would not break out, but he would also not give up.

That was why he was clinging to a pipe after having climbed up the chain hand over hand, to investigate what the ceiling had to offer. In particular, he was interested in the large cooling fan attached there, which sat above the door.

The chain he climbed was padlocked to the length of metal strut that supported the heavy machine and he felt the whole structure shake with every pull he gave.

Tanner guessed the machine weighed over three hundred pounds and despite the fact that sixteen separate screws, washers, and nuts held it to its support strut, the strut itself was attached to the ceiling by only eight long bolts, two of which were ready to fall out, while three of the remaining six were loose.

Not too surprising, Tanner thought, because he had been listening to the frequent rumble of subway cars since entering the room and had surmised that train tracks laid on the other side of the basement wall.

Years, and possibly decades, of day and night vibration generated by the trains had caused the bolts to loosen. Several years more would likely cause the machine to come loose and fall from its perch.

Tanner went to work accelerating that process. He'd been blessed with a bit of luck when he discovered that the inside diameter of the chain links fit snugly over the hexagon-shaped heads of the bolts and could be used like a wrench.

And although it took hours and left his fingertips raw, when he climbed back down the chain he was no longer just a beaten man awaiting his execution, but rather, he was a man with a plan.

2

SUICIDE OR DEATH

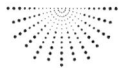

Tanner had been locked inside the freezer for the better part of a day when Sara returned and peered through the tempered glass, which was set at eye level in the door.

Tanner had considered breaking the glass earlier, but the slot was too small to reach an arm through and the glass was reinforced with a wire mesh.

During her absence, Tanner had relieved his bladder and watched the liquid flow down the drain beneath the long table, but with no food or water, he had wondered if Sara had simply left him alone to die of thirst.

When he finally heard the door that led down to the basement squeak upon opening, he got into position. He was standing back against the opposite wall where she had previously seen him, and except for the handcuffs laying open on the floor, he looked as defenseless as the last time she saw him.

Sara's eyes widened when she noticed that his hands were free, but she entered without hesitation and Tanner saw that she was holding a gun.

He was about to kill her when she did something that made him stay his hand. After opening the door and stepping into the room, Sara leaned down and slid her gun across the floor to him.

"I know you have no reason to trust me, Tanner, but I'm hoping that you'll at least let me talk, that you'll hear me out and… I'm hoping you won't kill me."

Tanner stared down at the gun and then back up at her face. She looked like hell and he wondered if Johnny Rossetti's death was the cause of it, or… was there something else?

Tanner was standing with his arms up and was grasping the chain. He tightened his grip and spoke.

"What's going on, Blake?"

Sara looked down at the gun and her face showed surprise that he hadn't reached for it, but then she met his eyes.

"I want to make a deal."

"What deal? And why should I ever trust you again?"

"I could have opened the door and shot you to death or just left you here to die, but instead, I gave you my gun. Doesn't that tell you that I'm serious, desperate even?"

"All right, what's the deal?"

"Your life in exchange for your help. My sister, Jenny, she's being held for ransom by a group of religious extremists and I want you to get her back, to free her. If anyone could do it, it would be you."

Tanner adjusted his grip on the chain again, as he pondered her words.

"Where is she being held?"

"She's… she's in Guambi."

"Guambi?"

"It's a small country located—"

"—near Indonesia, I know, and these aren't normal kidnappers, are they?"

"No, they call themselves the RRK, but it translates to the People's Freedom Fighters. There are estimated to be hundreds of them."

"You want me to travel halfway across the world, fight hundreds of armed men, and free your sister. Is that the deal you're offering? It sounds more like a suicide mission, and anyway, isn't it something the government should be handling?"

"The State Department is in talks with the government there, or rather, what's left of the government, but the people that have Jenny, my sister, they've already killed two hostages. Tanner, they hacked them to death with machetes… and time is running out."

"Why should I care what happens to your sister? And you've already proven that you can't be trusted."

Sara stared at him with defiance in her eyes. "I could have killed you and I didn't. I also gave you my gun as proof of my sincerity. I love my sister, Tanner, and you're the only one I know who would even have a chance of getting her back. If you want me to beg, I'll do it."

"Come here."

"Why?"

"I'll consider the deal, but I want you to come over here now."

Sara hesitated for just a second, then walked over and stood before Tanner with a questioning look in her eyes.

He let go of the chain and the massive cooling fan swung down from the ceiling and smashed the spot Sara had been standing on.

The sudden noise and crash of metal frightened her, and she grabbed onto Tanner's arm without realizing it.

"Good God! That could have crushed me."

"That was the plan," Tanner said, as he picked up the gun with one hand and grabbed Sara by the neck with the other.

Sara swallowed a cold lump of fear, as she looked into Tanner's eyes. "You're going to kill me anyway, aren't you?"

"You stuck a gun in Laurel's mouth and your own lying lips got Johnny killed."

Sara's legs gave out as she began to sob. Tanner released her and watched as she slid down to the floor. Her crying was harsh and made of her face an ugly mask as she fell over onto her side while gripping her hair, as if she meant to rip it from her head.

Tanner stared down at her in bewilderment. Sara Blake was one of the toughest people he had ever known and the only one ever to best him, even if her method to accomplish the task was unconventional. To see her fall apart was unnerving, and he found his hatred for her dissipating, to be replaced by pity.

Nearly a minute passed before Sara sat up against the wall. She wiped away tears and mucus with the sleeve of her blouse. After swallowing several times to clear her throat, she gazed up at Tanner with a sorrowful expression.

"I loved him, Tanner. I loved Johnny and because of me, he's dead. My sister, Jenny, she always said that my hate for you would destroy me, and she was so right, but it destroyed Johnny as well. I'm not sure that I can live with that, so if you want to kill me, just kill me… it's what I deserve."

Ten full seconds passed before Tanner spoke. They were seconds in which his finger twitched twice upon the gun's trigger, but did not squeeze it.

He nodded toward the cooling fan. "We'll have to

crawl over that thing to get out of here, so I hope you have the key for these leg irons."

Sara stared up at him for a moment, before reaching into a pocket of her jeans. She then removed the key, leaned over, and freed Tanner from the shackles.

When she stood, she touched Tanner on the arm.

"Will you help me get my sister back? I'll pay you anything you want."

"All I want right now is food and a shower, but you can tell me everything you know about what happened to your sister after that."

Sara headed for the door. "I have a car outside; we'll go to my apartment."

Before he could comment, Sara had climbed over the fallen cooling fan and was headed for the basement steps. Tanner followed, but he looked back at the place he thought he might die in, had expected to die in, even after rigging the machine to fall. Sara could have shot him the instant the door opened, or simply never have returned and left him to die.

Tanner took a final look, then he followed Sara up into the fading light of a day he thought might be his last.

3

SURREAL

Tanner stayed in Sara's shower a long time, as he washed away the grime of the freezer.

While on the way to her apartment, she had ordered food from a favorite restaurant of hers that offered delivery, and Tanner had eaten steak, along with a salad and baked potato, after first downing four bottles of water.

Sara had left him alone after the food arrived. He had eaten while gazing about at her apartment and asking himself why he agreed to help her, why he hadn't just killed her and escaped his prison. He had no answers for himself, but the image returned to his mind of her sliding her gun toward him. He knew the act had taken courage but must have been fueled by desperation.

There were family photos all along the hallway leading to the bedroom. He spotted several where Sara and a woman with blonde hair were smiling together. He surmised from the strong resemblance that this was the sister she hoped to save.

He had failed to save his own sisters, but like Sara, he had risked his life to save someone he loved, to save Laurel

Ivy, and like Sara, he had given up his weapon and surrendered to an enemy he knew would kill him.

That they were both still alive was against the odds, but the odds seemed greater still that her sister could be found inside a vast jungle and then rescued. However, he had beaten the odds his entire life and hoped to do so once again.

In the bedroom, atop a side table, there was an unframed photo of Sara with Johnny Rossetti, and yes, they appeared to be in love. Yet, it was her hate that had caused Johnny's death. Tanner knew that Sara blamed herself for Johnny's demise, and rightfully so.

After taking a long, hot shower, Tanner left Sara's bathroom wearing only a towel around his waist. She entered moments later carrying packages.

When she spied the stitched-up wound on his left side, she made a face.

"I heard you'd been shot. That's not infected, is it?"

"No, only reddened from the hot water, but I should cover it with a fresh bandage."

"I have some in the bathroom," Sara said and after walking into the room that was still steamy from Tanner's shower, she returned and told him to raise his arm.

While applying ointment and a bandage to his wound, Sara stared up into Tanner's eyes and saw that he was giving her a strange look.

"This is all a bit surreal, isn't it?" she said, and Tanner grunted his agreement.

When she finished with the bandage, she pointed at the bags she had piled atop the bed.

"The small bag contains a toiletry kit, while the big bag contains new clothing. Everything is in the sizes you asked for and they'll be delivering the suitcase and the rest of the supplies to the airport within the next hour."

"When will the plane be ready?"

"It's a private jet and it will be taking off for Jakarta in three hours."

"It's a long flight. How many stops will we make?"

"Just one before we land in Jakarta, we'll be refueling in South Korea and after that, we'll have to spend the night in Jakarta."

"And from there we go to Guambi?"

"No, the airport there is closed, but the resort we'll be staying at in the neighboring country of Telunas will fly us from Jakarta on their plane. It's a tight schedule, but we should make it."

"I see."

Tanner opened a bag and took out a pair of jeans.

Sara spoke from the doorway. "I'll be out on the balcony."

Tanner answered her with a nod and Sara left the room.

When he joined her twenty minutes later, he was wearing the new jeans along with a black long-sleeve T-shirt, and he had shaved as well.

The city was ablaze with artificial lights and the cacophony of sounds it produced drifted up to them from the busy streets below.

Tanner poured wine into a glass and sat across from Sara in a wicker chair.

"Tell me everything you know about what happened to your sister."

After sipping her own wine, Sara spoke.

"Jenny runs a non-profit organization and was there on a humanitarian mission. The government had recently stabilized, or so it seemed, but rebels still loyal to the old leader killed the new president and plunged the country back into civil war."

"You said that they were religious extremists?"

"Yes, and it's the extremists who were responsible for the anarchy and assassination, but the U.S. State Department informed my father that they weren't certain if that core group was behind all the kidnappings."

"Why the doubt?"

"The group is fractured, most of them are driven by their idea of religion and practice it fanatically, but then there are those committing kidnappings as a way to enrich themselves."

Tanner nodded. "I see, both groups ask for money, one to get rich and the other to fund their ideals. If that's true, then there's probably no way to know who has her."

"Yes, but I pray that the extremists have her. Their religion is very strict in matters dealing with sex... which means she's less likely to have been raped."

"How much is the ransom?"

"Ten million."

Tanner cocked an eyebrow at the figure. "Your family has that kind of money?"

"We can raise it, yes, but it will take time, and during the last conflict in the country, it sometimes took months before they released the hostages, even after the ransom had been paid. They were also known to arbitrarily kill hostages for reasons only they understood, but it was usually when the hostage had offended them somehow, such as the men whose bodies were found. They were gay."

"And once the ransom is paid, they ask for more, right?"

"Yes, and again, sometimes, they just, just kill their hostage."

The doorbell rang, and Sara stood. "That's Duke, please don't harm him; he was only following my orders."

Sara waited for Tanner to reply, but he said nothing. After sighing, Sara went to open the door.

Duke's eyes grew wide with fear as the door opened. Tanner reached past Sara and pulled the older man into the apartment, then tripped him. As Duke fell onto his back, Tanner placed his gun against Duke's forehead, right above the broken nose he had inflicted upon him in their previous encounter.

"Please don't kill him, Tanner," Sara said.

Tanner ignored her and spoke to Duke. "You do things for her. From now on, you'll also do things for me. Do you understand?"

"I do," Duke said, and Tanner was impressed that there was no tremor in the man's voice.

Tanner put the gun away and Sara helped Duke from the floor.

"I'd much rather work with you than against you, Tanner," Duke said.

Tanner raised up a finger. "For me, you'll work for me, not with me."

"Whatever you say, I'm just glad you two aren't still trying to kill each other."

Sara suggested that they move back onto the balcony. Once there, Duke told them what little he knew.

"As you can guess, Guambi isn't exactly a place where I have a lot of contacts, so the two of you will be going in blind."

Tanner stared at Sara. "The two of us? You're not planning on coming along after we get there, are you?"

"Of course, I am. This is my sister we're talking about, and I think you know that I can take care of myself."

"Yes, you can, here in the city, but the jungle is different. As a woman you won't be able to keep up."

Sara's eyes blazed. "That's sexist!"

"No, that's a fact and simple physiology. I'm faster than you, Blake. My legs are longer, and I have greater stamina. I may need to cover long distances quickly without resting, and if I do, you won't be able to keep up."

Sara made a face of displeasure, followed by a nod of assent. "That's all true. I may lag behind, but I'm still coming with you to find my sister. I'll be responsible for myself. Your only job is to find Jenny and get her to safety, agreed?"

Tanner didn't appear pleased, but he nodded in agreement and spoke to Duke.

"Fine, now what about weapons?"

Duke grimaced. "I do have contacts in Jakarta through an old friend. He says that the con artists and thieves in the region outnumber the legitimate gun dealers. So be advised, my friend says that this arms dealer in Telunas can be trusted, but not always, and that you'll have to check your weapons carefully to make sure he's not trying to sell you junk."

"That's not reassuring," Tanner said.

Duke shrugged. "It is what it is."

"How well armed are the rebels?"

Duke brightened, as he rubbed his palms together. "There's one piece of good news there. When they attacked the capital, they were unable to breach the armory and the military there remains loyal to the government. Few of the rebels will have guns and most of them will be armed with machetes or knives."

"What about the passports?" Sara said.

Duke reached into an inside pocket of his suit coat and his hand emerged with an envelope that contained two complete sets of phony IDs.

He laid them out on a glass-top coffee table before

Sara and Tanner. After reading them, they both jerked their heads up and asked Duke the same question.

"We're supposed to be married?"

Duke grinned. "It will arouse less suspicion."

His hand went into a side pocket and this time it emerged with two gold bands.

"I guessed on the sizes; I hope they fit."

They tried the rings on and saw that they were about the right size, then they both removed them until they would be needed.

Duke typed on Sara's laptop for a few moments and brought up a map of Guambi. Afterwards, he pointed toward a large section of the northwestern part of the nation, which was bordered on two sides by the Indian Ocean and the country of Telunas.

"It's believed by some that most of the rebels are based in this area, although satellites have been unable to verify that, and they'll likely move their camp frequently. Aside from the kidnappings, they're also suspected of pirating small pleasure craft. The area is just a mess right now."

"How do we get to Guambi, by plane?" Tanner asked.

"The airfield is still closed, and the State Department is advising all Americans to stay away, so you'll have to travel in on foot. This chaos all broke out while Sara's sister was in the air. If she had left a day later, her flight would have been cancelled."

Duke looked up from the screen and stared at both of them.

"What you two are planning to do is hopeless. A native of the country would have a problem locating the rebels. And if you did find a group of them, there's no guarantee that they would be the ones that took Sara's sister."

"What do you think Jenny's odds are, Duke?"

Duke sighed loudly. "The truth, fifty-fifty, and that's

only because your father is willing and able to pay. Most of the time, the negotiations fall apart because the rebels ask too much, but luckily for your sister, your old man is loaded."

"I'm not willing to sit back and just hope for the best," Sara said, then she looked at Tanner. "I studied you when I was tracking you down and over the last few weeks I've seen you do some incredible things, including today inside that freezer. If anyone can find and free my sister, it's you."

Duke looked at Tanner and then Sara. "What happened inside the freezer?"

"Tanner got free from the cuffs and rigged a trap. Once I stepped inside, he could have killed me."

"And she could have stayed outside the freezer and shot me to death, but she didn't," Tanner said. "Instead, she gave me her gun."

Sara leaned toward him. "I need you to trust me again. I really think you're the only chance my sister has."

"I'll do my best, Blake, but honestly, a team of mercenaries might be a better option."

Duke cleared his throat. "Not so, I heard a news report on the way here. The father of one of the other hostages is Conrad Burke, as in Burke, the multi-national, the defense contractor. He allegedly assembled a team of ten men and sent them in after his youngest daughter. One of them stumbled out of the jungle today with third-degree burns and said that they were ambushed and slaughtered, as far as they know, he was the only survivor."

"An ambush that was set up that quickly tells me they have eyes everywhere," Tanner said.

Duke nodded in agreement. "Yeah, Burke's group had been headquartered in the neighboring country of Telunas, which is where you'll be staying after your night in Jakarta, at their resort area. The extremists are gaining ground there as well. Someone on the hotel staff, a taxi driver, or even someone at the airfield could have tipped the rebels. Trust no one."

Tanner pointed at the map. "From what part of the country was Blake's sister kidnapped?"

"She and two other hostages were at a relief center in the eastern part of Guambi," Duke said.

"How certain are you that she and the other hostages are being marched northward?"

"I'm not certain at all. This is all just extrapolation from known facts, but the mercenaries were attacked north of the area where the hostages were taken, which does indicate that they're moving in that direction."

"That's good; it means that we'll have a chance of intercepting them."

DUKE WISHED THEM LUCK BEFORE LEAVING, AND SOON after, Tanner and Sara left the apartment and climbed into the limo that would take them to the airport.

Sara offered Tanner her phone. "Do you want to call someone, maybe Laurel?"

"No."

"Why not? You should let her know you're alive."

"I'll do that if I live through this. Otherwise, what's the point?"

Sara turned in her seat until she was facing him. "You'll find my sister and then we'll go our separate ways. I hated you for a long time, Tanner, but I never doubted your abilities. I locked you in a room with your feet shackled and your hands cuffed behind your back and I returned to a death trap. Most men would have surrendered, one or two might have gotten free of the handcuffs, but only you could turn the tables like that. Use that devious brain of yours to find my sister and bring her home."

Tanner said nothing in return and Sara shifted back in her seat until she was staring forward once more. Five minutes passed before she spoke again.

"I don't hate you, not anymore. I don't have the strength for it and it was my hatred for you that caused Johnny's death. I have to live with that."

She cried softly as Tanner watched her impassively, but as the taxi drove onto the Grand Central Parkway, he offered some advice.

"You've stopped hating me, now stop hating yourself."

"That's easier said than done," Sara said.

"Yes, but then, what isn't?"

Sara pondered those words, and despite her somber mood, she smiled.

4

WHEN IT RAINS

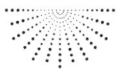

Laurel Ivy opened her front door before Joe Pullo could ring the bell.

After Pullo entered, they hugged each other in greeting and Laurel noticed that Joe held her longer than usual. When they separated, she searched his face.

"How was your day?"

"Insane. With Johnny gone, I'm running things and there's a lot I don't know. I spent most of my life on the streets. I'm not a manager."

"Has there been more trouble?"

"No, which I find odd, but I'll take the break."

Laurel took his hand and began leading him toward the kitchen.

"I'll heat up some food for you."

Joe pulled her back and searched her eyes. "How are you doing? I mean, we have to assume that Sara killed Tanner, and I know you loved him."

Laurel looked away for a moment as her eyes grew moist, but when she looked back at Joe, she gave his hand a squeeze.

"I don't know if Tanner is dead, but I do know that he loved me, loves me, and knowing that… it's freed me from the past."

"What do you mean?"

"For years, I thought that maybe I had fooled myself into thinking he loved me. Now that I know he did, I also realize we never would have lasted, not if he could feel that way about me and still leave me."

"And if he's alive… if he wants you?"

Laurel smiled, then kissed Joe. "I'm with you now. Tanner is part of my past."

Joe hugged her again. "I don't know what I'd do if I lost you too. First Johnny, and now Tanner. Laurel, do you think Tanner could still be alive?"

"I do. He's already come back from the dead once, and until I know differently, I'll assume he's out there somewhere."

Joe looked toward the kitchen. "I'm not really hungry."

Laurel smiled. "Let's go to bed."

Joe's phone rang. When he looked at the caller ID, his face paled two shades.

"This can't be good news."

"Who is it?"

"Sam's nursing home."

Joe answered the phone, and as the caller spoke, Joe's shoulders sagged, and he lowered himself to take a seat on the stairs.

"I understand, yes, thank you and… um, I'll be there in the morning."

When he put away the phone, Laurel saw that he looked utterly lost.

"Joe?"

"Sam's dead. They say he died in his sleep. Oh Jesus, Laurel, I'm losing everyone."

Laurel sat beside him and hugged him, as Pullo cried fresh tears of grief.

DUKE STEPPED OUT OF HIS VAN IN FRONT OF HIS HOME IN the Park Slope section of Brooklyn and felt the barrel of a gun get jammed against his ribs.

"Take the wallet, hell, take the van, the damn thing isn't worth my life."

"Is he dead?"

The female voice surprised Duke. When he turned his head, he saw Sophia Verona.

"Tanner is alive, I swear."

"Where is he?"

Duke turned to face her and smiled. "Right now, I'd say he's cruising at about forty thousand feet."

INSIDE A PRIVATE JET, TANNER, HIS OWN EYELIDS HEAVY from lack of sleep, stared across the aisle at Sara's slumbering form. As young as she was, she had already lost two lovers, and now there was a good chance she would lose her sister as well.

Tanner believed her when she said she no longer hated him and assumed that her passion for revenge had died along with Johnny Rossetti.

He kept staring at her and asked himself again why he hadn't killed her. The only answer he could come up with was that he respected her.

Sara had bested him, pure and simple, despite the method employed. He was only still alive because she had decided not to end his life.

He would find her sister, free her from her captors, then consider the slate clean between them.

Tanner drifted off to the first sleep he'd had in nearly forty-eight hours, as the jet he rode in drew ever nearer to danger, and possibly, the greatest challenge of his life.

5

IN THE JUNGLE, THE MIGHTY JUNGLE

IN THE JUNGLE REGION OF GUAMBI, JENNIFER BLAKE looked up at the noon sun and thought that she would pass out if they didn't stop to rest soon.

She was one of six hostages being held by a group of nearly three dozen men, most of whom were armed only with machetes, or goloks, as the locals called them. They had already proven that they would use the weapons, because when they started out, there were two more hostages.

The men had been a couple on vacation at the resort in Telunas, a gay couple named Philip and Lawrence, who were well educated, and both Australians in their thirties.

When the so-called freedom fighters realized the men were homosexuals, they had beaten them mercilessly before hacking them to death with the machetes.

It was the most horrific and inhumane sight Jennifer had ever witnessed, and it made her vomit what little food she'd had in her stomach.

The brutality had sickened and dispirited her fellow remaining hostages as well, for it had shown them that their lives could end at any moment, ransom demands or not.

Philip and Lawrence had been successful businessmen and their lawyer, or solicitor, would have gathered the ransom money and paid for their release within a day or two.

However, their captors found the men's obvious love for each other an affront to their religious beliefs. They forfeited the ransom for the opportunity to "cleanse the world of them" and would simply increase their ransom demands for the remaining hostages.

Besides Jennifer, there was a young woman named Melissa Burke. Melissa was eighteen and the daughter of Conrad Burke, whose mercenaries were bested earlier that day.

Burke's men had been expected and had walked right into a trap near a stream, where nets were dropped upon them and then set ablaze. The men fought back by emptying their guns in all directions, but they couldn't fight the flames and soon succumbed to the fire.

Jennifer had hugged the ground along with the other hostages when the fighting began and wondered if any of them would survive the rescue attempt.

When the conflict ended, they were all herded away through the jungle as fast as they could move, which wasn't very fast, because they were paired off and lashed together at the ankles.

Jennifer was bound to Melissa with a piece of coarse rope, while the other four hostages were likewise tied together.

There was a married couple from Florida named George and Reba Hough, who had been on their honeymoon in Telunas, when they were kidnapped while shopping at the marketplace in Guambi. They were in their fifties and the marriage was the second one for each of them.

The final two hostages were both men, a man of Asian heritage with the improbable name of Juan Rio, who was also a native-born Brit. Juan reverted to a Cockney accent when agitated. The other man was a pediatrician, Dr. Bill Washburn, who was black and a Canadian citizen.

Juan Rio was an engineer who had been working in the area, but both Melissa and Dr. Washburn had accompanied Jennifer to the country as volunteer workers for the charity she ran. She felt responsible for their safety, even though none of what was transpiring was her fault.

The leader of their captors was named Firman. He was a very thin man with wiry limbs and lots of dark hair, a beard, and bushy eyebrows.

Firman's religious zeal seemed evident, but Jennifer knew that some of the men serving beneath him were more interested in the money the ransoms would bring and had hopes of somehow getting their hands on it.

Dr. Washburn was an army veteran who had served in East Timor during the turn of the century. He had absorbed enough of the area's local languages to understand snatches of conversation between the men guarding them. From one of those conversations, Washburn learned that at least two of the men believed they should keep the money for themselves and not pass it along to fuel their cause of a separate nation. Washburn had also gathered that he and his fellow captives were being marched toward the rebel group's main camp, where they would likely be placed in a pit until their ransoms were paid.

Firman raised a thin arm in the air and gave the signal to rest, as they came upon one of the many streams that ran through the jungle.

Jennifer and her companions all sighed with relief, then they lowered their faces to the water and drank as well as they could by using one hand to brace themselves, while the other was cupped and brought water to their lips.

When they were done, they all stepped into the stream to cool off and bathe. They assumed the break would be a brief one, since they had lost time the day before, when they had to seek shelter from an afternoon storm.

The men removed their shirts, but the women had to wash while keeping their clothes on. Firman grew angry over any exposure of their bodies. At a previous stop, he had given the order that Mrs. Hough be beaten for removing her blouse, when she tried to make it easier to clean herself.

When Mr. Hough charged at the man who had struck his wife, he received his own beating and both husband and wife bore bruises.

Most of the rebels were young and the youngest of the separatists, a boy who appeared to be no more than sixteen, was named Prendy.

Prendy had taken a liking to the petite and beautiful, raven-haired Melissa. As she and Jennifer stepped from the water, he handed Melissa a piece of durian, a fruit that was native to the area.

Melissa thanked him with a smile and Prendy nodded shyly and moved away. Melissa then handed half of the fruit to Jennifer.

"Thank you, honey," Jennifer said, as she eyed Prendy.

Jennifer ate the small piece of fruit quickly, for although she loved the sweet taste and crisp texture, she found the fruit's odor unpleasant.

"Don't trust that boy, Melissa."

"Prendy? He's not like the others, and he has a crush on me."

"Just be careful."

Melissa sat next to Jennifer on the grass. "Do you think we'll be rescued soon?"

"I don't know. But I'm certain that both our families are busy making arrangements to pay our ransoms."

George and Reba both lay on their backs beside them, while Juan and Dr. Washburn sat across from them, and Juan asked Melissa what Prendy had given her to eat.

When she told him, he nodded and smiled. "That's good; you ladies eat as much as you can. All this bloody marching through the jungle can leave a person knackered. But Melissa, you watch that little bastard, he can't be trusted any more than the rest of these arseholes."

"Yes, Dad," Melissa said, and Jennifer and the others laughed.

Juan Rio was the father of four teenage girls, and he had been looking out for Melissa since their ordeal began.

"I'm not your bleeding dad, but I know a thing or two about the world, young lady, and that boy isn't giving you something for nothing, believe it."

"He won't… try anything. It's against their beliefs, right?"

The others said nothing, and Melissa suddenly looked worried.

6
EXTREMIST MAKEOVER

FIRMAN, THE LEADER OF THE MEN HOLDING JENNIFER hostage, rose from his prayer rug and sat on a straw mat beneath the shade of a tall tree.

As he turned his head to the left, his eyes fell upon the western hostages as they rested near the stream. A glare of distaste lit his features as he took in Jennifer's long blonde hair blowing in the breeze.

He then gazed about at his men and saw that many of them were eyeing Jennifer and Melissa. One in particular, the boy named Prendy, was eyeing the young girl as if he were a starving man and she was his only food.

After rising, Firman called over four of the men who he knew were fervent in their religious beliefs and as driven to rid their country of infidels as he was.

Once he reached the hostages, he studied Reba Hough, deemed her mouse brown hair to be short enough, and instructed the men who had been guarding the hostages to drag her and the males away. That left Jennifer and Melissa alone, and Melissa clung to Jennifer like a toddler clinging to its mother.

Firman barked orders at the four men he had arrived with and they pulled the women apart, as they each grabbed an arm and held them still.

As Jennifer and Melissa stood on their knees before Firman, he very slowly and dramatically removed his machete from its scabbard.

Jennifer was the first victim of the blade, as Firman yanked at her hair while hacking away like a madman.

When he was done with her, her hair was no longer than any of the men's and she had suffered several superficial cuts across her scalp.

Juan Rio called Firman a slew of names, and although the leader of the rebels didn't understand the Brit's words, he comprehended their meaning. With just a look in that direction, one of the guards smashed the flat of his machete across the back of Juan's head, which stunned the small man into silence.

Then, Firman went to work on Melissa, and she too was shorn of her locks and humiliated.

As the two women lay at his feet crying, Firman had to keep himself from hacking away at them.

As despicable as the creatures were, they would bring in a rich bounty from their families, then he and his brothers would be able to arm themselves with more than mere machetes.

Firman spat upon the women as a way to vent his hatred, barked out the order for his men to be ready to move in ten minutes, then strode back to settle upon his mat. As he sat there, he whispered the words of a prayer he had learned as a child.

7

AT LAST

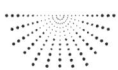

Tanner had been awake for an hour when Sara stirred and opened her eyes. When she looked over and spotted him, she startled, and he saw a look of fear expressed for a moment before she became fully awake.

She sent him a weak smile. "I have to get used to being near you."

"Without wanting to kill me, you mean?" Tanner said.

"Or fear being killed by you," she said.

They sat in silence for twenty minutes, until Sara broke it.

"My sister was like a second mother to me as I was growing up and I love her more than anything."

"She's older than you?"

"Yes, by six years and she's always been the wiser of us and the most kind." Sara stared at Tanner. "Do you have siblings?"

"They're dead."

"They must have died young."

Tanner nodded, and Sara saw that it was not a subject he was willing to talk about.

"The last time I spoke to my sister I called her a liar, because she told me that Brian once made a pass at her. I couldn't accept that she was telling the truth then, but I see that I was idealizing him. I loved him, still love him, but he had his faults and… his actions were partly to blame for his death. Had he never gotten involved with Richards, you two would have never crossed paths."

Surprise registered on Tanner's face. When Sara saw it, she curled her lips in a smile.

"Yes, I actually said that."

"Then I'll say this, I'm sorry that things went the way they did, although, if I hadn't killed him, someone else would have."

"Is that how you justify what you do?"

"No, Blake. I don't need to justify what I do. I kill for money, for those who can't or won't do their own killing. I consider it work like any other profession."

"But you could do other things, Tanner; you're certainly intelligent enough. Why kill for money?"

"We all do what we're driven to do, and I'm the best at what I do, not many people can say that."

"And you enjoy it, the violence, the killing?"

"I'm not a sadist, nor does it sexually arouse me, but I've a natural proclivity for the work. And yes, I do enjoy it. It's often challenging, even demanding, and what you've asked me to do is the greatest challenge yet."

"I haven't hired you to kill anyone."

"Haven't you? Or do you really believe we can free your sister without taking a single life? You may not know their names, but there are men alive right now in Guambi who will be dead when we leave there, and they'll be dead because you've hired me to kill them, even if you are only paying me with my life and not money."

Sara thought that over, saw the truth of it, and even took it one step further.

"Some of those men may have women who love them and I'm bringing you there to kill them, which will cause those women grief… the same as your killing of Brian caused me grief."

"If that bothers you, we can turn the plane around and go back to New York."

Sara shook her head. "Kill as many as you need to, but I want my sister free and safe."

"And Frank Richards wanted to stay free and safe when he asked me to kill Brian Ames. I'm a tool, Blake. A gun for hire, and now I'm working for you."

They were silent again, but Sara soon shattered it by voicing an observation.

"It's a shitty world where a man can make a career of killing other men for money."

Tanner smiled. "At last, we finally agree on something."

8

GIRL TALK

Laurel lit up in a huge grin as Sophia delivered the news.

Joe had been getting ready to go to Sam Giacconi's care facility when Sophia called. Joe asked her to come by Laurel's townhouse. She told them her news over coffee taken at the kitchen table.

Tanner was alive.

"This guy Duke says that Tanner and Blake made a new deal. She lets him live and he saves her sister from the rebels in Guambi."

Joe scratched his chin as he digested the news. "That sounds like it could take a while. He could probably search that jungle for weeks and never find her."

Sophia smiled. "This is Tanner we're talking about; he'll find her."

Laurel let out a deep breath. "This is such a relief; I was so afraid he had sacrificed himself to save me, but Sara must have come to her senses."

"That bitch doesn't have any sense," Sophia said. "She just needs Tanner's help more than she needs to see him dead, but no matter the reason, it means he'll be coming back someday."

"I hope it's soon," Joe said, and there was such despondency in his voice that it caused Sophia to look at him carefully.

"Something else has happened, hasn't it?"

"Yeah, Sam Giacconi died."

"Oh Joe, I'm so sorry."

"Thanks, but now it means that I have two funerals to plan, for two Dons, and God, I miss both of them more than you know."

Sophia smiled. "When Johnny and I first started going out he was intimidated by you, and then he told me a couple of weeks ago that you were his best friend."

Pullo looked startled. "He said I intimidated him, why?"

"You had a rep as a hard ass, still do, and Sam was always praising you. Johnny looked up to you and wanted to be like you."

"Hell, he surpassed me, and he was twice as smart as I'll ever be."

Laurel leaned over and kissed him on the cheek. "Don't underestimate yourself, Johnny didn't. It was why he made you his advisor."

Sophia shook her head sadly. "We lose a lot of good people too soon in this life."

Joe nodded in agreement, while fearing there would be more losses in the coming days. When he offered to walk Sophia out, she declined, while saying that she wanted to stay and visit with Laurel.

"A visit?" Joe asked.

"Yeah, girl talk, you know?"

Joe looked at Laurel. "Is that all right with you?"

Laurel smiled at Sophia. "Yes, I think we should get to know each other better."

Joe left after giving Laurel a kiss goodbye. Laurel asked Sophia to follow her back into the kitchen, where they settled at the table over more coffee, along with chocolate croissants.

Sophia, not one to beat around the bush, came right to the point.

"Tanner was willing to sacrifice himself for you and I know you've got the hots for him. So tell me, what's going to happen when he comes back?"

Laurel sipped her coffee before answering, and after placing her cup down atop the table, she leaned back in her seat and stared across at Sophia.

"I love Tanner and have since the moment I first laid eyes on him. At the time, I cheated on my husband to be with him. That was then and I'm a different person now."

"You're saying you don't want him?"

"I love Tanner, but I can't have him, and I'm not sure any woman can, because I think there's just something in Tanner that won't allow him to be intimate. He fears love, you should understand that if you're serious about him, but I also think he has feelings for you."

"Why do you say he has feelings for me?"

Laurel gave a little shrug. "I've seen you two together, and I hope it works out for you, I really do. But I'm with Joe now and although I'll always love him, Tanner and I will never be together again."

"Does Joe know that? Because I have to think he's as worried as I am about what happens between you two when Tanner returns."

"We've talked about it. I told him that I don't want Tanner and that I want him."

"Talk is cheap, and with all he's lost lately, I'm sure Joe

wouldn't mind a little extra reassurance that he's not losing you too."

Laurel gave that some thought and nodded. "You're right; I should leave no doubts in his mind."

Sophia stared at her and made a face. "Damn."

"What's wrong?"

"I like you, Laurel, and I didn't want to."

Laurel grinned. "That makes two of us."

9

THE ONE AND ONLY

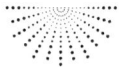

Refueling in South Korea took longer than expected due to an instrument in the cockpit needing to be replaced. Because of the delay, the accommodations at the hotel in Jakarta had been given away to a foreign news crew covering the story in Guambi. Sara realized that she and Tanner had nowhere to stay once they landed. To make matters worse, a new storm was blowing into the region and would be going strong by midnight.

Sara had received the news about the lost hotel rooms after they made their stop for fuel, and she became busy making calls to find a solution but came up empty. She kept trying, but when they were minutes from landing, she admitted defeat.

"I don't know what to do. One of the people I talked to said that the planes were being grounded tonight, that's how bad the storm will be. I suppose we'll just have to sleep in the airport terminal."

Tanner held out his hand. "Let me have your phone."

Sara gave it to him, but she asked a question.

"You know a place where we can stay?"

"I do, but you'll have to behave while we're there."

"What's that mean?"

"It means that you keep your remarks about me to yourself. If you insult me in front of these people, they'll toss you overboard."

"Overboard? They have a boat?"

"Yes, a cabin cruiser."

"Who are these people?"

Tanner had put in the number. He was about to press send when he looked up and stared into Sara's eyes.

"They're the closest thing I have to family."

AFTER LANDING, THEY WAITED OVER AN HOUR FOR THE TAXI to arrive, then spent nearly two hours navigating through traffic that made rush hour in New York City look tame by comparison. By the time they reached the dock it was past noon, and they were both tired and hungry.

Sara saw her first. She was a small brown woman with a wide smiling face and glittering dark eyes. She was running at Tanner at full speed. When she reached them, Tanner opened his arms and the young woman leapt into them as if she were a child.

"Xavier! You've come home!"

"It's good to see you, Nadya," Tanner said, and the smile on his face was wide and genuine.

As her feet touched the ground again, Nadya smiled at Sara. "This is your friend, Xavier?"

"Her name is Sara Blake."

Nadya stared at Sara, then back at Tanner, and a sly grin came across her face. She then hugged Sara as if she were a long-lost sister. So genuine was her affection that

Sara hugged her back, even as she mouthed a question to Tanner.

"Xavier?"

He nodded.

A man came toward them with a smile as wide as Nadya's had been. He was white, about six feet tall and his blond hair reached his shoulders. His skin told you that he had spent a lot of time outdoors, for while he was not as naturally dark as his wife, Nadya, his hide was still bronzed from the sun.

As he drew closer, Sara could see that beneath the tan there were faded tattoos on his arms. When he reached them, he and Tanner hugged like brothers.

The man lowered his sunglasses and Sara saw a pair of brilliant blue eyes, she also saw that the man was looking her over as if he were taking inventory.

"Shit, Xavier, she's too damn hot for a mutt like you."

"She's… just a friend, and her name is Sara Blake. Sara, this is Romeo."

"Romeo?" Sara said.

Romeo grinned. "The one and only, baby."

10

HOPE

JENNIFER THOUGHT THE BREEZE FELT ODD AS IT BLEW across her shorn scalp, even as the sun burned patches of flesh that had never felt its hot caress.

She and Melissa both looked like victims of a mad hairstylist, and both bore bald patches along with scabs where Firman's careless cutting had left a nick.

Melissa's shorter hair hadn't seemed to dull Prendy's fascination with the girl. The young rebel still eyed her as if she were the loveliest thing he'd ever seen, despite the grime covering her face and the filthy twill pants and sweat-stained blouse she wore.

Jennifer trudged along with Melissa at her side in synchronized steps that were becoming second nature, as the two women were still bound together at the ankle with rope.

The coarse cord had caused both their ankles to redden and then bleed, but after so many miles, there was just an awareness of pain there that bordered on numbness, like a minor headache that irritates but doesn't disable you.

They were in the middle, with Juan Rio and Dr. Washburn in front of them and the Houghs behind them.

Jennifer had tried to keep track of what direction they were traveling in, but what trail existed meandered and they would frequently move east or west to pick up a new one, often in an effort to avoid an army patrol that one of the advance scouts had seen.

Wherever they were being taken, she expected it to be no better, and wondered if her father had arranged for her release. Would she be set free, or would Firman simply kill her once the money was paid?

They came to a sudden stop. Jennifer heard Melissa inhale sharply, and when she followed her gaze, she saw the three dead bodies sprawled across the trail.

The dead men looked like rebels, with their well-worn khaki pants and baggy tunics, and when Firman turned one over, Jennifer realized that they were the men sent forward as scouts and that her captors now numbered three less.

A second later and Firman was shouting orders to his remaining men, and while a dozen of the men paired off and went to search the surrounding jungle, Prendy and the others that remained herded them over to a group of trees and kept guard over them.

Juan Rio whispered. "It looks like they have trouble. Hopefully this is another rescue attempt."

Dr. Washburn looked doubtful. "One of those men was stabbed from behind, while the other two were slashed across their throats. I can't be certain, but it looks like one man killed them."

One of the guards turned and screamed at them to be quiet and they complied. They knew from experience that there would be no second warning, only violent reinforcement of the command.

Still, they all looked at each other with emerging smiles, as they dared to hope that a rescue was forthcoming.

11

BRO

PHOENIX, ARIZONA, SEPTEMBER 1998

Cody Parker, going by the name of Xavier Zane, sat on the edge of his motel room bed and fought back tears as he thought about his slain family, who had been murdered one year ago to the day.

His best friend and mentor, Tanner, had offered to stay with him and talk, but Cody declined the offer while saying he'd be fine.

But he wasn't fine and despite his inherent toughness and stoical nature, he found himself becoming lost amid dark thoughts, memories of the final moments of his loved ones' lives, and Cody was feeling more than a touch of survivor's guilt.

The three loud knocks on the door roused him from his despair and, after wiping away a stray tear, he rose, looked through the peephole, and sighed.

The door opened to reveal the smiling face of Romeo, who was holding a bottle of liquor. The mellow and carefree boy wasn't alone. There were two girls with him, both young and beautiful. After looking Cody over, the one on the right sent him a huge grin.

"Xavier, say hello to Carla and Alicia."

Before Cody could say anything, Romeo brushed past him while holding Carla's hand. Alicia, the girl who had been on the right, was now standing alone in the doorway. Cody ushered her in with a sweep of his arm.

"I'm Xavier."

"I'm Alicia."

The girl was a blonde with huge green eyes, and when she walked into the room as if floating on air, Cody intuited by her lissomness and grace that she was a dancer.

Romeo draped an arm over Cody's shoulders and held up the bottle. "We're going to have a drink or two, get to know each other, and then go out and light up the town. What do you say?"

Cody managed to break free of Alicia's gaze, and after turning his head, he whispered to Romeo.

"Didn't Tanner tell you that I wanted to be alone?"

"Yeah, but he didn't tell me why," Romeo whispered back. "But hey, bro, nobody wants to be alone, not really, and I'm just looking out for you."

Cody sent him a small smile. "Bro?"

"Hell yeah, we're like brothers, aren't we? And Tanner, he's like our old man."

Cody's smile widened, he then looked back at Alicia and the beauty sitting on his bed grinned again.

"Romeo, I owe you one, bro."

"All right, now let's get this party started."

SARA, AND ROMEO'S WIFE, NADYA, BECAME FAST FRIENDS AS the foursome ate and relaxed in the lounge of the cabin cruiser. When Sara realized that Tanner was known to them by the name, Xavier Zane, a light of recognition dawned in her eyes.

At one point, Nadya and Romeo went into the galley, leaving Tanner and Sara alone.

"There was a hired killer out west years ago that went by the name of Xavier Zane; I'm going to assume that it's not a coincidence."

"It was me," Tanner admitted.

"And is that your real name?"

"No."

Sara gave a little shake of her head. "How young did you start?"

"It doesn't matter," Tanner said and there was a touch of anger in his voice.

Sara said, "I was just curious," and then Nadya slid into the booth and sat beside her again.

"I want you to come shopping with me, Sara, and then these two can catch up."

"Okay, and there are a few items I need."

Nadya smiled at Tanner. "I like her, Xavier. You have good taste."

"You're way off base, Nadya; there's nothing between us."

Nadya waved that off. "You forget my gift; I know these things."

"Gift?" Sara said.

Romeo took a swig of beer, then smiled at his wife. "Nadya is psychic."

"Really?" Sara said, and the doubt in her voice was plain to hear.

Romeo laughed. "Don't believe, I didn't at first, but I'll

tell you this, she told me last week that Xavier here was coming to visit soon and now here he is. She does shit like that all the time. It's spooky."

"Interesting," Sara said, but the doubt was still evident in her tone.

WITH THE WOMEN GONE, TANNER AND ROMEO moved above deck and drank beer beneath a sky that was growing dark with the approaching storm.

"Are you really not sleeping with Sara? Because that is one beautiful woman, bro."

Tanner told Romeo about the history between him and Sara, and Romeo shook his head.

"You always did have a way with women, and hey, what about the old man, have you gone to see him lately?"

"No, I haven't seen him. Why, is there a problem?"

"Nah, and we'll be visiting him next year... after the baby is born."

Tanner had been raising his beer bottle to his lips, but he paused halfway. "Baby?"

"Nadya's pregnant, bro, three months, you're going to be an uncle."

Tanner reached over and shook Romeo's hand. "I'm happy for you."

"And what about you, you ever think about settling down?"

Tanner shook his head. "It's not for me."

"I said the same shit for years and now here I am with Nadya. Who knows, maybe someday you'll fall in love again."

Tanner said nothing, but his thoughts turned to Laurel Ivy.

12

DEEP

Ten thousand miles away from where Tanner sat with Romeo enjoying an evening drink, Laurel Ivy was in her kitchen preparing coffee to start the day.

Joe came down the stairs and Laurel left the kitchen to greet him with a kiss.

"Have breakfast before you leave."

"I should get going; I've got a long day ahead of me."

Laurel took him by the hand. "All the more reason to have a good breakfast."

Joe let her pull him along toward the kitchen. With Sam Giacconi dying on the heels of Johnny Rossetti's murder, he had decided to hold both funerals on the same day. He now faced the chore of having to arrange two burials, while also running the day-to-day affairs of a crime syndicate and preparing for the possibility of war with the Russian mob.

Once they were in the kitchen, Joe just stood there with his brow creased in worry.

Laurel gave his hand a squeeze. "You've got a lot on your mind, don't you?"

"That's an understatement, and I'm not sure I'm cut out to be Don. I was fine running crews, but now I run everything."

"Isn't there someone you trust and who you can delegate some of your responsibilities to?"

"Maybe, I'll have to give that some thought. Right now, I've got to make sure we're prepared for war, because the Russians will be making a move soon, I just know it."

Laurel kissed him on the lips. "Have faith in yourself. I do, and I know you'll come out on top."

"Thanks, baby, I hope you're right."

As Laurel began cooking, she spoke over her shoulder. "While you're at the club, I'll be meeting with the funeral director this morning and making arrangements. I'll call you if I need your help in deciding about something. Oh, and Sophia said she would come along and help me. Wasn't that nice of her?"

Joe turned around in his seat. "You'll really do that? There are a lot of details and it's not exactly fun."

Laurel leaned over and kissed him. "I'm here for you, baby, you know that."

No, Joe hadn't known that. Despite what Laurel had said the other night, Joe had been fearing that their relationship would be ending soon, now that Tanner had confessed his love for her and would likely return soon.

Joe gazed up at Laurel and spoke in a hoarse voice. "Thank you, that will really help."

Laurel reached in her pocket and took out a key. "That's for the front door. I think it's time you had one, don't you?"

Joe took the key, and as he stared at it, he sat straighter and his chin lifted. He then stood and took Laurel in his arms. As the embrace ended, he touched her on the cheek.

"You're sticking with me, even though you know that Tanner loves you?"

Laurel smiled. "I love Tanner, you know that, but what we had, that's in the past… I love you now, and I think that we can have a future, don't you?"

Joe grinned. "I love you too, Laurel. And yeah baby, you're the only one I want to be with."

They had just finished eating when the doorbell rang. It was Merle and Earl. Laurel greeted her brothers with a hug.

Pullo sent the boys a nod, then noticed that they were wearing suits.

"You guys came in the limo?"

"Yes, sir, and we'll take you anywhere you want to go," Earl said.

"You were Johnny's drivers, not mine."

Merle walked over and stood before Joe. "We're yours now, and since you and Laurel Lee are together, we'll help you any way we can. You don't even have to pay us or nuthin'."

Joe studied the brothers while he came to a decision. "All right, but I'll keep you on the payroll. I think I see now why Johnny liked you so much; there's more to you two than I thought."

Merle nodded in agreement.

"Earl and me, we're deep."

13

DAD

Half a world away from New York City, beneath an evening sky growing dark with rain clouds, Jennifer huddled together with Melissa and the rest of the hostages under a plastic tarp with holes in it. Even though they were sitting on its edges, the tarp threatened to blow away at any moment, as a storm raged around them, and the ground became muddy.

The women still had shoes, but not the men. The rebels had taken them for their own use on the first day, and George Hough, Juan Rio, and Dr. Washburn all had feet that bore many fresh scars and abrasions.

Their captors had built a series of lean-tos that sheltered themselves from the rain, but Jennifer and the others had to make do with the tarp and would soon be in total darkness when the last of the day's light faded away.

Melissa shivered despite the humidity. When Juan Rio removed his shirt and draped it around her shoulders, she thanked him profusely while assuring him that it helped.

The Asian man with the Hispanic name and the cockney accent was as different from her father as a man could get, but Melissa appreciated the fact that he was looking out for her as if she were his own daughter. She gave him a peck on the cheek.

"Thanks, Dad, and do your daughters know how lucky they are?"

"Those four are all teenagers; they won't appreciate me and their mum until they have kids of their own."

One of the guards pulled up a corner of the tarp and stuck his head under, then slid a piece of cardboard toward them that had brown rice piled atop it.

Everyone dug in like it was a gourmet feast, because it was the first food they had seen in nearly a day. There were no utensils, so they had to eat with their hands.

Once the food had been devoured, Juan Rio began talking, telling stories about his girls and their mother. At one point, he had everyone laughing so that the guard outside shouted at them and kicked at the tarp.

Dr. Washburn wasn't married, but he and his only sister were close, and he knew that she was probably worrying herself sick over what had happened to him.

That caused Jennifer to think of Sara. She told the group that she regretted arguing with her sister the last time they were together.

The Houghs had children, a son each from their first marriages. Both boys were away at college.

"We don't have any money, just a mortgage, along with tuition and car payments, but because we're Americans these devils think we're rich," George Hough said.

They all agreed that the ransom amounts were outrageous. Except for Jennifer and Melissa, there was no way the other families could raise such funds.

"Someone will rescue us," Dr. Washburn said, but there seemed to be no conviction behind the words.

A commotion began outside the tarp and George

Hough lifted a corner to peek out and see what was going on.

Dr. Washburn listened intently, and as he caught the gist of several conversations between their captors, he smiled.

"One of the men failed to return after going off to have a bowel movement and they found him dead. It seems that someone is stalking them."

The tarp was ripped away and the group was herded through the heavy rain and into one of the lean-tos. They were then guarded over by several men. Although no one spoke of it, they all had hope in their eyes.

14

TO HAVE AND HAVE NOT

Romeo's cabin cruiser had two staterooms, both with bathrooms, but Nadya insisted that Sara use the bathroom in the main stateroom, because it had a tub that she could soak in.

When Sara returned to the guest stateroom, she knew from the sounds coming from beyond the bathroom door that Tanner was showering.

When Tanner emerged two minutes later, he was bare-chested and wearing a pair of faded denim shorts that he had borrowed from Romeo.

Sara looked at him and then over at the narrow bed. "Um, about the sleeping arrangements..."

Tanner laughed. "Relax, Blake, I'll be sleeping in the lounge."

Sara sighed. "Good."

Tanner turned to leave, but Sara called to him to relay the news that she was able to confirm their accommodations at the luxury resort in Telunas. However, due to the storm, everything would be pushed back a day. The hotel in Telunas was apologetic but couldn't give them a room until a day later, because the storm would delay the departure of their current guests.

"Do you think that Romeo and Nadya will mind if we stay another day?"

"No, they both seem to like you."

"They love you, and you seem more human around them. Romeo calls you brother, but you're not related, are you?"

"Not by blood, no. And speaking of blood, it's a shame we're being delayed. I know you're worried about your sister and that you want to find her as soon as possible."

Sara looked shocked by his remarks. "Thank you, yes, I am angry at the delay, but there's little I can do about it. I'm surprised you're sympathetic enough to know how it would affect me."

"We scumbags have our moments," Tanner said, as he referenced the term she'd recently used to describe him.

Sara was about to respond, but Tanner turned and left the room before she could speak.

THE FOLLOWING MORNING DAWNED CLOUDY, BUT FREE OF heavy rain, as the storm moved slowly out of the area.

With their trip to Telunas delayed, Tanner went to work after breakfast and helped Romeo replace the carpet in the lounge. To his surprise, Sara helped Nadya clean and even polished the boat's brass railings and fittings.

By working together and skipping lunch, they had finished in time to enjoy an early dinner out. After returning to the boat, Romeo introduced Sara to a native beverage called arrack, which was Indonesian rum.

"It's very good," Sara said, after taking a sip.

"I have a buddy that makes this himself, and don't be fooled, it's strong stuff."

After talking for a while, Romeo and Nadya retired just after dark. They had volunteered to take Sara and Tanner to the airport in the morning and had to get an early start.

After they left, Sara excused herself, and Tanner was alone above deck. He awoke not realizing that he had fallen asleep and noticed two things. One, it was dark, and two, he was no longer alone.

Sara sat across from him with a nearly empty bottle of arrack, and she was smiling at him.

"You were snoring, but just a little."

"Did you drink that whole bottle, Blake?"

"Um-hmm, I like it a lot."

Tanner took a good look at her and noticed that her eyes were red, as if she'd been crying. She was still wearing the shorts and sleeveless top she'd worn earlier, but she was barefoot.

"What's wrong, did you get news about your sister?"

Sara hugged the bottle. "I called home and Duke said that Johnny's funeral is today. It's probably taking place right now."

She began to cry again, as she tilted the bottle up and drank the last few sips that remained.

Tanner stood, took the bottle from her, then beckoned her to follow him. Sara did so, but when she stumbled and nearly fell, he caught her.

"Everything's spinning."

"I know that feeling," Tanner said.

He led her past the galley and into the guest stateroom, pulled back the covers on the bed, and gestured for her to lie atop it.

Sara fell back onto the mattress with her head on the

pillow and stared up at him. "Stay, I don't want to be alone."

"How many bottles of that rum did you drink?"

Sara's face scrunched up in confusion, but then she got it. "No! I meant stay and talk, not, not here in bed."

"I know what you meant, Blake."

"Oh… but will you stay?"

Tanner settled into a chair. "I'll stay until you fall asleep."

Sara began crying again. "I loved Johnny, Tanner. I loved him, and I killed him. They say when you seek revenge to dig two graves, and I hated you so much that I would have died to see you dead, but I never would have traded Johnny's life for yours. My hate wasn't that strong. Jenny was right; I've screwed up my whole life by seeking revenge, now I have no career, no hope… and no Johnny."

A few minutes later, Sara had cried herself to sleep.

Tanner sighed. "Ain't love grand?"

15
DON PULLO

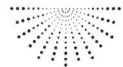

Robert Vance listened as Michael Krupin spoke to the crew leaders who would head the assault on the Giacconi Family's enterprises.

They were poised to attack and takeover the Giacconi drug distribution centers and chop shops. It would all take place simultaneously while most of the Giacconi Family's key players were at the cemetery mourning their two former Dons.

The Russians were holding the meeting inside a warehouse in Lower Manhattan, not far from the restaurant Krupin owned, and above which he kept an office.

Across the city, hundreds of Krupin's men waited to receive orders before heading to their targets.

The plan was to assault ten key locations with overwhelming force before moving on to the smaller targets and taking control of those as well.

Vance knew the media would be full of headlines and broadcasts screaming about a mob war, but by hitting hard and fast, the war would be over in a day. And with the

Giacconi leadership all gathered for funeral services, they would be taken wholly unaware.

Michael Krupin finished with his men, then he and Vance climbed back inside his limo.

"Everything's ready?" Vance asked.

"Yes, but I still have a concern."

"You're talking about Tanner, but as I told you, he's missing in action and from what little I've been able to learn, it had something to do with the same incident that killed Rossetti."

"Fine, and this Joe Pullo, you don't have any concerns about him?"

Vance laughed. "Pullo spent most of his life as a button man for old Sam Giacconi, he's only in charge because he's next in line. After the disaster he'll have today, it wouldn't surprise me if one of his own people kill him and take over."

Krupin checked the time on his Rolex. "In less than an hour, the city will be mine."

∽

The funerals were being held inside a venerable church, which was so crowded that many were forced to stand.

In an alcove, Joe and Sophia were speaking with some of the leaders of the other families, when Sammy Giacconi approached.

Sammy was wearing a suit, but had his long hair tied together and hanging down his back. When he spotted the redheaded Sophia, he froze in his tracks and stared at her while smiling.

"What are you looking at, kid?" Sophia said, even as her eyes roamed over Sammy in return.

"I'm looking at a dream come true," Sammy said.

Sophia smiled. "I see you have your grandfather's silver tongue, but I'm a little old for you and too much woman."

"You look just right to me," Sammy replied, then he walked up to Joe.

Joe had seen Sammy earlier after entering the church, but he hugged the young man again and asked him how he was holding up.

"I'm good, Uncle Joe, but I do have a concern."

"Speak your mind."

Sammy gestured out toward the gathered mourners. "Is this a good idea, I mean to have everyone here like this? What if the Russians attack us today?"

Joe sent Sammy a reassuring smile as he reached over and straightened the young man's tie.

"It's all right, Sammy. Things are under control."

Sammy shrugged. "Okay, but it makes me nervous."

Sammy's concerns were proven valid while they were at the cemetery, because as the burial services for Johnny Rossetti and Sam Giacconi ended, Pullo looked around and saw that most of his lieutenants were answering their vibrating phones.

Each of the men oversaw a division of the Giacconi Crime Family and had come to pay their respects to two of its former leaders.

Security was tight, and the press was being kept back, but were still visible beyond the police barricades.

Joe gestured for the other men to follow him as he walked toward a tent he had ordered be erected, so that he could assure some level of privacy away from telephoto lens and the eyes of the authorities.

Sammy came over, but two bodyguards at the tent's entrance told him to leave. He looked past them and called to Joe.

"Uncle Joe?"

"Let him in, boys."

Sammy entered the tent and looked around at all the men studying their phones. "What's going on?"

"The Russians are attacking," Joe said.

Sammy's eyes brightened with alarm. "What do we do? What about our people? Where are they attacking?"

Joe smiled. "Calm down, Sammy. I'm not the sharpest knife you'll ever find, but I did learn a few things from your grandfather. We were ready for this."

"What's that mean?"

"It means that those locations are empty. Vance, the man behind the Russians, he had knowledge about us from another man named Heinz. If he had moved on us sooner, he could have hurt us badly, but he wanted to be slick and hit us today while we were at the cemetery. It made sense because so many of us are here and would have trouble responding to an attack, but Sam taught me a long time ago to think like my enemy, and like you, I saw this coming."

Joe called over one of the men who was staring alternately at his phone and the second hand on his watch. He was a burly man with gray at his temples.

"Let Sammy take a look, Al."

Al angled his phone so that Joe and Sammy could see what was playing on it. It was a soundless video feed from what just hours earlier had been a drug distribution warehouse but was now an empty building.

There were over a dozen men with guns wandering around inside the building and one of them was talking into a phone.

Inside his limo, Michael Krupin was speaking to the man on the other end of that phone and learning that they had been outmaneuvered. It was the third such call he had taken in the last thirty seconds.

Krupin looked over at Vance. "Another location found empty. It looks like Joe Pullo isn't the simpleton you thought he was."

Vance cursed wildly in Russian, but he stopped in the midst of his rant as a thought came to him.

"Get everybody out of those buildings. Do it now!"

Back at the cemetery, Sammy listened as Al counted down from ten and noticed that most of the other men were doing the same thing, as they looked at the feeds coming from other locations.

"Three, two, one," Al said, and when Sammy stared down at the phone, he saw a bright flash before the video feed ended.

The other men were all smiles, and many laughed, before all of them looked over at Pullo with eyes full of respect.

Sammy let out a little laugh of his own, as he realized what had just happened.

"You blew them up, didn't you?"

Pullo looked at him with a solemn expression. "The Russians wanted war, they've got one."

Al put his phone away, dropped to one knee and spoke two words. "Don Pullo."

The other men followed suit, but as Sammy began to lower himself, Joe took him by the elbow and stopped him.

Joe spoke to his men. "This was just the first battle, and we'll not only win this war, but I plan to take back the territory we lost in the last one. The Russians are going to learn that no one fucks with the Giacconi Family."

The men rose to their feet while cheering as Joe turned and spoke to Sammy.

"Johnny once told me that he thought you were the future of the family, and I think he was right. I want you by my side from now on. What do you say to that?"

Sammy's grin was as wide as any Joe had ever seen.

"Yes, Don Pullo, and those Russian bastards will wish they had never born."

16

A FAMILIAR FACE

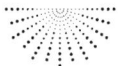

Tanner and Sara arrived in Telunas and checked in at the hotel as Mr. and Mrs. Robert and Linda Coleman.

Their suite was large but had only one bed. Sara stared down at it as they entered the bedroom to unpack their bags.

"I guess it's my turn to sleep on the sofa," she said.

"Suit yourself," Tanner said, "but that is a large bed."

"You mean share it?"

"I won't touch your goodies, Blake. I'm not a rapist."

Sara thought about the sofa she'd seen in the other room and then stared down at the king-size bed. Although she had been in the area for days, she was still feeling the effects of jet lag and thought the sofa wouldn't be nearly as comfortable as the bed.

"We'll try it, and I never thought you were a rapist."

"Just a scumbag, hmm?"

"Yes… but, maybe I was wrong about that."

Tanner cocked his head. "What have you done with the real Sara Blake?"

Sara attempted a smile, but it faltered before it could even form.

"I'm not sure who I am anymore. A part of me died with Brian and another part has died with Johnny. My whole life is now about getting my sister back, and after that, well, I don't know."

"It gets easier," Tanner said.

"What does?"

"Surviving loss, but the key is to keep moving forward."

Tanner's words intrigued Sara and she gazed up into his eyes. "Who have you lost?"

Tanner broke eye contact and walked over to the phone. "I'm hungry, what about you?"

Sara accepted the abrupt change of subject and shook her head no. "I will take coffee, though, and maybe a croissant if they have them."

Tanner called room service, then the two of them unpacked their things in silence.

JENNIFER'S GROUP HAD PAUSED IN THEIR TREK TOWARD THE rebel camp as Firman sent his men out to find and kill whoever was stalking them, after more men failed to return from a patrol.

The clouds had dissipated by first light, allowing the blazing sun to return and bake them. Jennifer was grateful that Firman had moved them near the edge of a stream where they had ready access to water.

There were three guards keeping watch over them, with the young Prendy being one of them. Jennifer had caught him staring at Melissa several times as if he were imagining her naked.

The boy wanted Melissa, that was obvious and Jennifer worried that he would attempt to take what he wanted, whether such an act was against his religion or not, for in truth, they were all little more than slaves to their captors and certainly at their mercy.

Juan Rio wiped the sweat from his brow. "It's hot here, but I could use the rest. I'm not used to walking this much."

Both of the Houghs nodded in agreement. They were about the same age as Juan and Dr. Washburn, but not as fit. The rugged daily march toward the rebel camp had been toughest of all on the newlywed middle school teachers.

Juan leaned in and spoke softly to the others. "Who do you think is out there? I think it's one or more of those mercs that tried to rescue us the other day."

"I pray it's the Marines," George Hough said.

"It's one man, that's my guess," Dr. Washburn said, and the rest of them nodded in agreement, because they knew that he had combat experience.

"So, what do you think, mate?" Juan Rio said. "You think he'll just keep pecking away at them until only one is left?"

The doctor had opened his mouth to answer when the guard to their left cried out in pain. Melissa screamed when she saw the knife handle protruding from the rear of the man's neck, as he fell to the ground at their feet and twitched violently.

Prendy must have seen where the knife had come from, because he fumbled at the pistol on his belt before firing wildly into the trees on the left, where a figure had turned and darted back into the shadows.

Jennifer had caught a fleeting glimpse of the man

before he dove for cover, and her mouth dropped open in shock as she realized it was a face she knew very well.

The man had been Jake Garner, her lover, and he was doing his damnedest to save her.

17

AN ARMY OF ONE

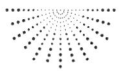

Jake Garner ran as fast as his legs would allow, as a smile lit his face with joy.

He had spotted Jennifer, had seen that she appeared relatively unharmed, and had also managed to kill or seriously wound another one of the men holding her for ransom. If he could stay alive and free for another day, he felt as if he would have a chance to rescue her.

He heard at least three men behind him and swerved toward the trap he had set up. The country of Guambi was riddled with streams, had several rivers, and was bordered on one side by the Indian Ocean.

Many of those streams only gain life during the rainy season, which can last for months some years, but when that season ends and the streams run dry once more, they still leave their traces behind in the form of long sandy troughs.

Jake had spent time before the attack on setting up a trap, by sharpening the ends of branches with a machete, and then burying them in the bottom of a trough with their pointy ends facing up. When he was done, he covered the handmade spears with palm fronds to obscure them.

Jake had used this same trick to kill three other men and he was using it again, but with a twist.

After coming to the trap, Jake made a long leap, ducked low, and then lay on his stomach to hide among a collection of thick plants that gave him cover.

When the three guards came rushing along in his wake, Jake watched as they slowed to a skidding halt in front of the scattered palm fronds. Apparently, they had heard of the way in which their compatriots had been wounded for slaughter.

One of the men crouched down while the others looked about. When the man brushed aside the fronds, he saw the sharp spikes sticking up from the bottom of the trough.

All three men let out a laugh. When their friend had stood again, they backed up, took a running start, and jumped over the spikes. Unfortunately for them, upon landing on the other side, they broke a thin, almost invisible thread of fishing line, which freed several tree branches with still more spikes tied to them. As the branches whipped around, they embedded their spikes into the men's faces, necks, and backs.

As the men cried out in agony and shock, Jake sprang up, rushed toward them and began hacking away with his machete.

He tried his best to make each blow a fatal one; however, one of the men struggled and thrashed around so much that Jake had to inflict over a score of wounds until the blade finally slashed across the man's throat and he bled to death.

Jake looked at the horror he had wrought on the rebels

and dropped to his knees and vomited the spare bits of raw fish and roots he'd been sustaining himself on.

He had never killed anyone before coming to Guambi, but he knew he would slaughter as many men as it took to free Jennifer. Still, he would never get used to it and the violence sickened him each time he employed it.

Before leaving the scene, Jake reached over and freed the gun hanging low on a man who had taken spikes to the left eye and jugular vein. When he checked the revolver, he saw that it was fully loaded. Then, he ran toward the nearby river as fast as he could, as the shouts of yet more rebels filled the jungle air.

18

WHAT GOES UP

Tanner and Sara had changed clothes and walked about the resort to blend in as tourists, while hoping to discover if there had been any new developments.

After calling home, Sara learned that the rebels had contacted her father and increased the amount they demanded for Jennifer's release. Sara's fear for her sister's welfare also increased.

Soldiers seemed to be everywhere in their gray uniforms, to comfort fears and keep the tourists' dollars flowing in Telunas, which really was a beautiful place.

The resort was painted in blue, green, and pink pastel colors. It was beautifully landscaped and offered over a mile of white sand beach with turquoise water and an awesome view of sunrise each morning.

After hanging around the hotel bar, Tanner had uncovered a piece of news that the resort management was trying to keep under wraps. An American staying at the hotel had gone missing, but was assumed to be lost, rather than kidnapped. At least that was the story being offered.

Sara had been upset by the news that another

American had gone missing, surprised when informed that the man was an FBI agent, but outright flabbergasted when she heard the man's name.

"Jake Garner? Are you certain?"

"Yes," Tanner said. "That's what the bartender said. Wasn't he your partner, the one you shot?"

"He and Jenny are dating, and I accused him of using her as a way to get back at me. I thought he would break her heart, but if he's here, then… he must actually love her, to risk his life this way. My God, have I ever been right about anything?"

"You think he's out there trying to rescue her?"

"Yes, Jake is much too smart to get lost. He's either out searching for Jennifer… or he's been captured too."

"Maybe we can contact him, or even call him if he's carrying his cell phone and is near a cell tower, but I've heard that the typhoon that passed through the area recently destroyed many of them."

"I still have his number on my phone. I'll try calling when we go back to the room."

"There's one more thing. The army is placing troops at the border between Telunas and Guambi. That will make it more difficult for us to leave the country."

"That's an understatement, but we have to find a way around it."

"First, we'll need weapons; do you have the money and the directions to where the meeting will take place?"

"Yes, and it shouldn't take us long to get there."

"I want to make a stop at the hotel gift shop."

Sara looked surprised. "The gift shop, why? Are you buying something for Romeo and Nadya?"

Tanner smiled. "Not exactly."

SUICIDE OR DEATH

WHILE THERE WERE ARMY TROOPS KEEPING PEOPLE AWAY from the Guambi border, no one spotted Tanner and Sara as they left the resort grounds and moved farther down the shoreline, where a huge sign written in over twenty languages warned that leaving the resort area was not a good idea.

Sara walked along at his side empty-handed, but Tanner carried a white cardboard carton under one arm that was about the size of a hat box. It was sealed on the top and bottom with a wide strip of clear tape.

As they came around a curve in the shoreline, they saw the other face of Telunas, as miles of shacks, shanties, and downright hovels went on for as far as the eye could see, with only a short line of homes in the distance that looked new.

The people wore little clothing and what they owned was faded and tattered. Young children ran about naked and there was smoke rising in the air from numerous cook fires.

"This is horrible," Sara whispered.

"As bad as it is, it was worse before the resort was built."

"You've been here before?"

"Yes, I passed through a long time ago, but there were no houses at all then and no chance to make a real living. Still, like every other business, I'm sure the resort doesn't pay their people any more than they need to."

Three men walked toward them from the shacks. All three were shirtless, looked tough, and long-handled goloks hung in sheaths fastened around their waists by rope.

Tanner sighed as he realized they weren't carrying anything. "This was a waste of time; they don't have any weapons."

"Maybe they're in the waistbands of their pants,

behind their backs."

"Possibly, but not likely."

Sara looked at the box Tanner carried. "It's a good thing you came prepared."

"Yes, and be ready."

As the men reached them, the one in the middle, the smallest of the three, spoke to them in English with a strong Dutch accent, while pointing at the box Tanner carried.

"You bring money, good."

"Where are the weapons?" Sara asked.

The man laughed at her and spoke to Tanner. "You let woman speak for you?"

"She's not my woman; I'm working for her."

The man swiveled his head to take in his companions and saw that they were laughing as hard as he was. He then called Tanner a name that would roughly translate to the English word, wimp.

Tanner waited until the laughter died down and then spoke.

"Give us the weapons and we'll give you the money."

"Why is money in a box?"

"It's for the weapons, we'll need something to carry it all in. We're buying four handguns and two boxes of ammo, no?"

The man's smiled widened. He slid out his machete as he and the other two men drew closer.

"No, give me box."

"You're robbing us?" Tanner said, and his tone was one of incredulity.

The punk called him a name that insulted not only his intelligence but also his manhood and grabbed the box. After shaking it and hearing paper rustling, he sat it atop the sand, then knelt and tore the box open.

When the multi-colored balloon flew up into the air, all three men followed its ascent with their eyes. That gave Tanner and Sara the opportunity they needed to strike.

While Tanner kicked the kneeling man hard in the mouth with his booted foot, Sara connected with the crotch of a second man.

The third man had his machete free and was raising it to strike when Tanner dropped to the sand and rolled into him, which caused the man to fall face forward.

By the time he hit the sand, Sara had gathered up the machete that belonged to the group's leader and was holding the blade against the throat of the man she had kicked in the balls.

As the man who had fallen got back up, Tanner tossed sand into his face and blinded him, then wrested his machete away. The leader rose as well, and his mouth was covered in blood.

After mumbling curses at them from lips that hurt more than his wounded pride, the man and his companions followed Sara's orders and trudged back toward the shantytown, minus their machetes.

Tanner plucked the bundles of cash that were laying loose inside the box and handed them to Sara. Afterward, the two of them walked away without the guns they needed.

"We'll have to come up with a plan that doesn't involve weapons," Tanner said.

Sara turned her head and smiled at him. "That trick with the balloon, did you learn that at hit man school?"

"Why, they don't teach that at Quantico?"

Sara laughed as Tanner smiled, and they walked the rest of the way back to the resort in companionable silence.

19

CALL ME SARA

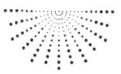

"I have an idea," Tanner said, as he and Sara sat at a table inside the hotel's bar.

"What's your idea?"

"Instead of going to the rebels, why not let them come to us?"

"What do you mean?"

"I mean we'll play the part of the rich American couple and let everyone know we have money. It'll be like sending up a flare to the rebels. Once they kidnap us, we'll eventually wind up at their camp."

Sara smiled. "And Jenny will be there too, but we'll still be hostages."

"And I'll still be me, and being me, I'll find a way to get us free."

"I don't know; it won't be easy."

"No, it never is, but we could wander the jungle for weeks and never find that camp. This way, we'll be taken right to it. You brought me here because I'm good at surviving long odds and I don't intend to die here, but it's your decision."

Sara considered things for a moment and made a comment. "Even if the rebels come for us, they'll have the same problem that we have. They'll have to get past the soldiers guarding the border."

"They'll find a way. This is their turf, their people, and then there's always the option of a well-placed bribe. In a region this poor, corruption is a certainty if you know the right people."

"All right then, what do we do?"

Tanner smiled. "We act like a couple of rich assholes. In other words, just be yourself."

Sara scowled. "Just because I come from money doesn't mean that I'm a—"

She stopped talking when she realized Tanner had been teasing her, and then she laughed.

"Tanner?"

"Yes, Blake?"

"Call me Sara; after all, we are married."

"Whatever you say."

"And don't you have a name, a real name?"

"I did at one time, but now, I'm just Tanner."

Sara's face darkened. "Tanner, the killer."

"Yes, and the men who took your sister will be making my acquaintance very soon."

"I hope you kill them all."

Tanner smirked at her.

"What?" Sara said.

"I think you're getting your fire back. That's good, you'll need it."

"I still feel empty inside, and I miss Johnny more than I would have imagined. What do you think is happening in New York? Is Pullo capable of running the Giacconi Family?"

Tanner grinned. "Joe is more intelligent than he lets

SUICIDE OR DEATH

on. Vance and the Russians are probably licking their wounds by now."

∼

Michael Krupin was one angry young man. The twenty-three-year-old was used to getting his way and suffering a massive setback was not an event he coped well with.

Vance, who was known to Krupin as Rurik Varanov, watched the young man as he paced about the room and occasionally stopped to hurl something at the door. It occurred to Vance that Krupin wasn't fit to lead, and that the situation would have to be remedied soon.

There was another man in the room. He was nearing sixty and his hair had begun to gray, but he still had a young man's build and a military bearing. His name was Fedor, and he didn't bother to hide his disdain for Vance.

"Michael, I warned you that listening to this fool was a bad idea. Maybe now you'll take heed of what I say the way your father did."

Krupin pointed at Fedor. "I don't want to hear 'I told you so.'" Krupin paced back and forth once more and then spoke to Vance. "Eighty-two! Eighty-two men dead, over a hundred wounded, and you can bet that they'll try to trace them directly back to me. The Feds are getting involved. Did you know that? And they say they can't tie any of it to the Giacconi Family."

"I underestimated Pullo. I admit that, Michael, but I promise you that I won't do it again."

Krupin walked over to where Vance sat and screamed down at him.

"We had one huge advantage over them; we had more men, but not after today. God, this has made me look like nothing but a fool. You have to fix this, Rurik, and you have to fix this soon."

Vance stood suddenly, which caused Krupin to step backwards so quickly that he nearly fell. Standing to his left, Fedor placed his hand on the gun in his holster.

"I will fix this, Michael."

"How?"

"I'll kill Joe Pullo and then I'll work my way through their ranks until there's nothing left of the Giacconi Family but memories."

Krupin straightened his tie and calmed himself. "I think I like your plan."

Vance smiled. "I knew you would, and I'll start on it right now."

Vance left the office and Krupin settled behind his desk.

"Fedor."

"Yes, Michael?"

"If Rurik fails to kill Pullo, I want you to kill Rurik."

"Fine, but it would be better if I killed him in any event, no?"

Krupin gave that some thought. Vance had been a friend of his father and he had known the man since he was a boy, known him and liked him. When he didn't answer Fedor's question, Fedor spoke again.

"Michael?"

"Yes, kill him."

Outside the office, Vance removed his ear from the door and slipped away down the stairs soundlessly, as a look of hatred tainted his face.

20

WEAPONS OF MASS PROPORTION

As Tanner and Sara passed the front desk on the way to their room, the clerk informed them that the hotel manager wanted to see them in his office.

The subject of the meeting was described as "A minor problem with their accommodations," but after entering the room and being confronted with guns, Tanner realized the problem they faced was a major one.

Two men held weapons on them while a third sat behind the hotel manager's desk. He was not the hotel manager; his name was Conrad Burke. Burke was around sixty, looked fit and had intense brown eyes. Those eyes studied both of them with suspicion and curiosity.

Tanner and Sara recognized Burke from his recent televised visits to give testimony before the United States Congress about charges leveled against his company, which was one of the largest multinationals in the world, and bore his name, Burke.

Burke gestured for his men to bring them forward and soon they were seated in two chairs in front of the desk, but only after a pat down.

Sara had found the search for weapons invasive, as one of the men fondled her.

"Those are my breasts, not weapons," Sara said, and the lecherous guard just smiled at her.

The other man had detected the bandage on Tanner's left side. He tore open his shirt to inspect it, saw what it was, and grunted.

Once settled in his seat, Tanner spoke. "What do you want, Burke?"

"I want to know who you two really are."

Tanner looked over at Sara. This was her operation, but he saw no reason to hide their identities or intent from the father of one of the hostages, and the man could prove useful.

Sara sent Tanner a nod and then revealed the truth to Burke. When she was finished speaking, Burke tapped a few times at a tablet computer, before looking down at it and then up at Sara.

"Yes, I see the strong resemblance between you and the other Miss Blake." He then looked over at Tanner, who was wincing in pain while rubbing a hand over his bandaged wound. "She said your name was Tanner, but what's your first name?"

"It's just one name."

Burke studied him through squinted eyes. "My father once hired a man named Tanner to handle a problem for him, but that was over thirty years ago, and I happen to know that man is dead. So what does that make you, Tanner number six?"

Tanner held back his surprise at Burke's knowledge and answered the question.

"I'm the seventh Tanner."

Burke made a face. "You don't deserve the name. The

other Tanner never would have been taken and controlled so easily."

"You're probably right," Tanner said, and launched himself atop the desk while freeing a slim blade he kept hidden in the folds of the bandage.

The weapon had a ring on one end that slipped over a finger and an inch-long blade with a razor-like edge. It was flexible but sharp, and Tanner laid it against Conrad Burke's throat as he wrapped an arm around the man's neck.

Sara was as surprised as everyone else in the room, but when she saw that the guards were bringing up their guns, she grabbed the bottom of her seat, lifted it up and placed a chair leg back down atop the instep of the man who had fondled her.

The man howled in agony as he instinctively dropped his weapon and grabbed for the chair, but Sara had already left it, to dive to the floor and retrieve the fallen gun.

The other guard had his weapon trained on Tanner, but Sara was pointing his partner's gun up at him and the man knew that no matter what happened, if violence came, he would die.

"Tell your man to drop his gun, Burke," Tanner said.

Burke was swallowing hard but had otherwise stayed calm. "Wilson, holster your weapon."

Wilson did as commanded, but he kept a wary eye on Sara, who was rising to her feet. Meanwhile, the other guard had taken Sara's vacated seat and was removing his shoe to check on his damaged foot.

"Mr. Tanner?" Burke said.

"What?"

"I apologize for doubting your abilities and I do believe

that we all want the same thing, yes? We want to see the hostages freed?"

Tanner slid off the desk and stood. "We should work together, and I have an idea how we can do that."

"I'm listening," Burke said.

"You have resources we don't. Can you get your hands on a small GPS tracking device, something that can be embedded beneath the skin?"

"I could have such a device here in hours."

Sara spoke to Tanner. "You want him to be able to track our movements so he can send help when we reach the rebel camp?"

"Yes, of course that assumes we'll be taken as hostages like the others were."

Burke nodded. "It's a good idea, and if it works, I'll send in more men to back you up. But, tell me something, Tanner. Without that help, what exactly were you planning to do against what must be over a hundred men?"

"I was going to do my best, Burke. Up until now, it's always been enough."

Burke laughed. "You're a cocky bastard. I like that. And you Miss Sara Blake, you are one brave woman to risk yourself this way."

"Not brave, desperate. I have to get my sister back."

"We will. By working together, we'll get her and Melissa back safely."

They made plans to meet again, and as they turned to leave, Tanner looked down at the man sitting in the chair, whose foot Sara had damaged, and who was also the man who had fondled her in the guise of checking for weapons.

"Let me see your hands."

The man gave Tanner an odd look, but he raised his hands up tentatively.

As they were still rising, Tanner gripped the fingers of

both hands and twisted viciously, which caused several digits to become dislocated. The man howled in fresh agony as hot tears fell unbidden from his eyes.

Tanner glared down at him. "That will teach you to keep your hands to yourself."

Tanner left the room and Sara followed with a wide grin on her face, while fighting the urge to laugh.

21

WEIRD

That night, Tanner had showered first and was lying in bed wearing only a pair of black boxers, when Sara walked out of the bathroom dressed in silk pajamas, which bore a floral print.

The bed was large enough to accommodate three or four people if needed, and Tanner was perched on the far side, near the windows that overlooked the pool.

Sara walked over to the bed, looked down, and shook her head. "This is too weird."

"I won't touch you, Blake. I promise."

Sara kicked off her slippers, lay down, and the soft bed felt so good that most of the tension left her body.

"I am tired, and still a little jet-lagged. Goodnight, Tanner."

"Goodnight, Blake."

Sara turned off the light, but despite being exhausted, she just lay there staring at the dark ceiling while listening to the sound of the central air unit and the infrequent footfalls and muffled voices, as someone passed by in the hallway.

She looked to her right and could just make out the shadowy shape that was Tanner. She recalled her hatred for him, the blind rage of vengeance she carried around night and day as she sought the man's death. Now, he was likely the only one who could find and rescue her sister.

"Are you asleep?" she whispered.

"No," Tanner said.

"Why didn't you kill me? I mean when we were inside the freezer. I know that you wanted to, so what stopped you?"

"I guess I let you live because you gave up your gun."

"Is that all?"

"Yes."

"I thought that maybe you felt sorry for me."

"You did look pathetic."

"Oh, thank you. That makes me feel better."

They were silent again, but Tanner broke it with a question.

"Will you be coming back to New York when we free your sister?"

"No. I need to get away, and my apartment holds too many memories. Memories of Brian, and now Johnny. And I need to figure out what to do with the rest of my life."

"That's simple; just take it one day at a time."

Sara smiled in the dark. "That's easier said than done, but then, what isn't, right?"

"Exactly."

"Goodnight again, Tanner."

"Goodnight, Blake."

"It's Sara; after all, we are sharing a bed."

"Goodnight, Sara."

Sara laughed. "This is so weird."

"Yes."

SARA AWOKE THE NEXT MORNING TO FIND HERSELF ALONE in the bed, but there was a note propped up on Tanner's pillow telling her that he would be back by ten a.m.

When he reentered the room at 9:46, Sara was dressed and on the phone with her father.

"I have to go, Daddy, but I'll call again soon."

After she ended the call, Tanner gestured at her phone. "Your family doesn't know that you're here, do they?"

"No, but if Duke doesn't hear from me for more than a month, he'll let them know what I tried to do… and that I likely failed."

"I was out looking for a way to get past the border and into Guambi. I had no luck since they doubled the number of guards on patrol. I guess it's time that Mr. and Mrs. Coleman made themselves very noticeable."

"And how do you suggest we do that?"

THE BARTENDER AT THE POOL WAS WORKING AS FAST AS HE could and was still having difficulty keeping up with the drink orders, as Tanner, in the guise of rich American Robert Coleman, was buying drinks for everyone.

He was also telling an endless parade of stories about his travels around the world and had caught the eye of several young ladies, even though his wife, Sara, known as Linda, was seated beside him in a chaise lounge.

One particular lovely was a French woman named Nicole, who carried on a conversation with Tanner in her native language. She giggled when she realized he had once eaten at her father's bistro. As she was leaving the table, Nicole whispered something in Tanner's ear, before sending a guilty glance toward Sara.

"You speak French very well," Sara said. "And did I also hear you speaking Italian?"

"Yes."

"You must have spent time in Europe."

"And so have you. I heard you telling that bodybuilder type about the German ski resort you liked so much; it sounded as if you had been there more than once."

"So, the Roberts are both well-traveled, flirts, and big spenders. That should attract attention. By the way, what did that French tart whisper in your ear?"

"She was letting me know what room she was staying in and that her friend would be out all evening."

"And will you be taking her up on that offer?"

"No, we shouldn't separate, or there's a chance that you'll be taken alone, and I'll return to find a ransom demand."

"I hadn't thought of that, too bad for you."

Tanner's eyes flowed over Sara in her red bikini. "Any man with a wife that looks like you would be staying in at night anyway."

Sara lowered her head and stared over the tops of her sunglasses. "Don't forget that this is all pretend, Mr. Roberts."

Tanner didn't respond, but there was a smile on his face.

22
JUNIOR

Michael Krupin kept an office above the restaurant he owned in Manhattan. It was there that he met with FBI agents, Tamir Ivanov and Justina Moretti.

Ivanov was the lead agent of the pair and was forty-two, while his young female partner was only twenty-seven. They were both in shape and dressed in well-tailored conservative suits that made them look more like businesspeople and less like the Feds they were.

Despite the Russian name, Tamir Ivanov was as American as could be. The Brooklyn born former New York City cop spoke his mind plainly, often too plainly, as the numerous reprimands inside his personnel folder could attest.

Tamir stood just short of six feet tall, had trimmed brown hair, and his ice-blue eyes seemed to look right through you.

Justina Moretti appeared haughty and just had that look that said bitch, although it was not her way and she was actually kind and unpretentious. However, nature had seen fit to have the beautiful woman with the lustrous dark hair broadcast that impression, and it did have its advantages in her line of work. She was also not averse to displaying a sharp tongue if provoked.

Fedor stared at Justina's ass as he followed them up the stairs to Krupin's office. Vance was leading the way, and when he opened the door, Ivanov and Moretti saw that Krupin had six lawyers present. The men were all lined up behind Krupin, where the young would-be King of New York sat at his desk with his palms lying flat atop the surface.

The agents also noticed that there were no other chairs in the room, except for the love seat against the right wall, and Vance and Fedor promptly occupied it.

Tamir smiled at Michael Krupin. "Hey there, Junior. I bet wearing the Daddy pants isn't as much fun as you thought it would be, hmm?"

Michael Krupin's brow furrowed. "Are you talking to me?"

"Yeah, and as far as I know, you're the only junior here. Mikhail Krupin Jr., son of Mikhail Krupin Sr., who was a former dirtbag commie and KGB agent. Your dad came here and went into the drug trade. He recently received payback in the form of a stroke, which I understand has left him a drooling vegetable."

Five of the six lawyers opened their mouths to protest, but Tamir raised a hand.

"You're right; I'm sorry, I should have said allegedly went into the drug trade. But we all know there's no doubt that the kid's father was a former KGB agent and a dirtbag, and I bet he drools on himself too."

Krupin's face reddened. "Who the hell do you think you're talking to?"

"He's talking to you," Justina said, and Krupin stared at her as if she had just appeared.

"What's your name? And what's his name? All I know is that you two are Feds."

Tamir told Krupin their names and the young man stared back at him in shock.

"You're Russian?"

"I'm an American, and like you, I was born in Brooklyn."

"You're still Russian."

"No boy, I'm a Special Agent with the FBI and I would like to know what you know about the men who got killed in those warehouses."

"I don't know anything."

"You're telling us that you don't know anything about those eighty-four men?"

"I thought there were eighty-two?"

"Ah, so you do know something."

One of Krupin's lawyers bent over and spoke in his ear.

"My lawyer has advised me to remain silent. I think I'll take his advice."

"That's fine," Tamir said, as he walked over and stared down at Vance and Fedor. "You two have anything you want to say?"

"We don't know a thing," Vance said.

"I know something," Fedor said, and Krupin squirmed behind his desk.

"What is it you know?" Tamir asked.

Fedor pointed toward Justina. "I know that she is one fine piece of Italian ass and I'd like to see her naked."

Krupin laughed nervously at that. He stopped when Tamir stared at him with his blue eyes of ice.

"Justina?"

"Yes, Tamir?"

"This old goat here would like to see you naked. What are the odds of that happening?"

"About the same odds as him getting hard without the help of a pill. It's always the ones with the limp dicks that talk the most."

This time Vance laughed, while Fedor cursed under his breath.

Tamir turned back to look at Krupin. "Okay Junior, you don't want to talk to us like a man, so I'll do the talking. We know that many of the dead men were employed by a security firm, and although we can't yet prove that you own the firm, we both know that it's true. All of the dead men were of Russian descent and most of them had arrest records. Overall, I'd say the city is a safer place. Still, it's my job to stop the violence from escalating, so I'm here to tell you to end the war and make peace with the Giacconi Family."

The most senior of the lawyers spoke up. Like Justina, the man gave off an air of haughtiness, but unlike Justina, his was well earned and practiced.

"My client knows nothing about the explosions, the warehouses, or the dead men, and he certainly has no knowledge about a 'mob war.' If you have nothing else to say, I suggest you take your leave."

"Your client is a punk who is in over his head. He'll likely be eaten alive if he continues to mess around with the big boys. And yeah, I think I'll go. Justina, do you have anything else you want to say?"

"Nah, as usual, you said it all."

They were at the door when Krupin called out to Tamir.

"Hey Fed, why don't you go harass Joe Pullo?"

Tamir turned back around and smiled at Krupin. "I'll be speaking to Mr. Pullo very soon."

"*Mr.* Pullo? Don't you have any cute names for him? Aren't you going to insult him the way you've insulted me?"

Tamir shrugged. "I doubt it. Unlike you, Joe Pullo has a pair of balls. While I still think the man is a criminal, he's not a namby-pamby little Daddy's boy like you are. Then again, you never know, the guy might rub me the wrong way."

Krupin's hands were still laying atop the desk, but they were balled into fists and shaking with rage.

"If you weren't a Fed…"

Tamir laughed. "Anytime Junior, bring it on anytime man to man and I promise you I'll leave my badge out of it. Hell kid, you must be twenty years younger than me. That might help you, but I doubt it."

Fedor stood, held the door open, and the sound of conversation and the tinkle of silverware drifted up from the restaurant below.

"It's time you two left."

"Whatever you say, gramps, and don't forget to burp the kid after you feed him. Oh, and change his diaper, will you? It smells like shit in here."

Tamir left with a laughing Justina at his side, as the sound of Krupin cursing in Russian filled the air.

23

DENY, DENY, DENY

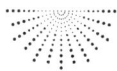

Tanner excused himself from the card game he was in as Sara pretended to nag him about his drinking. A short time later, they returned to their suite after a day spent playing rich and clueless tourists.

Sara locked the door and let out a sigh. "I think the guests and the staff certainly know we're here, but what do you really think the odds are that we'll be kidnapped?"

"I'm not sure of the odds, but I say we give this some time before trying something else."

"Fine, but Jenny has been gone for days and I can only imagine what she's going through."

"It's the best I could think of, but there are no guarantees."

Sara stifled a yawn. "I'm tired, do you mind if I shower first?"

"No, and I'll be out on the balcony enjoying the quiet. Today was noisier than I'm used to."

Sara smiled. "I don't think you stopped talking for more than a minute."

"Yes, Robert Coleman is a big mouth with too many dollars and not enough sense."

"And what part was I playing?"

"You're my trophy wife."

Sara made a face. "I suppose that's better than being called the old ball and chain."

Sleep eluded both for a time, as they waited to see if their playacting would bear fruit. If it did, that meant they might be attacked and abducted at any moment.

"Tanner."

"Yeah?"

"Remember, don't fight back; just let them take us."

"Don't worry, and you try to appear afraid."

"I won't have to act, trust me."

"You're the bravest woman I know, Blake, and you're smart. If you weren't, I'd have killed you the first time I tried."

"I was just driven by hate and it made me too stupid to be afraid."

"We should get some sleep."

"Right, goodnight."

They became silent, but neither of them would fall asleep until more than another hour had passed.

After their visit to see Krupin, Tamir and Justina visited the Cabaret Strip Club, where Sammy Giacconi escorted the FBI agents into the office and offered them seats in front of Joe's desk.

Sammy was about to leave when Joe told him to stay.

The young man grabbed a folding chair and sat beside Joe behind the desk.

Tamir made a show of looking around. "Where are your lawyers, Pullo?"

Joe smiled. "Knowing those bums, they're probably out playing golf."

"Michael Krupin had six lawyers with him. What do you think of that?"

"I think I should have went to law school with suckers like Krupin around."

"I did go to law school and let me tell you, you didn't miss anything. Now, as you probably know, I'm here to ask you about the pipe bombs that went off inside the warehouses earlier this week. We have reason to believe that you were behind it. That also makes you responsible for the deaths of eighty-two men."

Joe said nothing and Tamir and Justina looked at each other.

"What do you think, Justina?"

"I think that Mr. Pullo is too smart to open his mouth and he doesn't need a lawyer to tell him to keep it shut."

"I agree."

Joe smiled at them. "You two want a drink?"

Tamir waved the offer off. "Since you won't talk, I will. It's believed that you and the Russians are involved in a turf war and that it was little Mikey Krupin that started it. We also believe but have yet to prove that you were behind those bombings and the deaths of those men. That said, let it be known that this sort of shit won't be tolerated by the Federal government and that if this war, vendetta, or whatever you want to call it continues, every effort will be employed to stop it."

Sammy spoke up. "How would you stop something like that?"

Tamir pointed at him, but he looked at Pullo. "Is he your kid?"

"This is Sammy Giacconi."

"The grandson? Well hell, kid, it looks like you've joined the family business."

"You haven't answered my question," Sammy said. "How would you stop a mob war? Because if you can stop it, why not do it now?"

Tamir looked at him for several moments and saw that the ice-blue stare wasn't working on Sammy the way it did on Michael Krupin. He leaned forward and spoke in a whisper.

"That's the kind of shit they teach us to say, but you and I both know that the war will end when one side wins."

Sammy smiled at him and Tamir leaned back in his seat.

"Our main concern is that no civilians get hurt," Justina said. "It's bad for the tourist trade, you know?"

Joe nodded. "My guess is that the only people who will be hurt are the ones that deserve it, but again, that would just be a guess on my part."

Tamir smiled at that before turning to his partner. "Anything else, Justina?"

"Nah, Joe there knows the score and he also knows that we'll be back."

Tamir stood along with Justina, but turned in the doorway, as Sammy held it open for them. He gestured around at the office.

"You're a Don now, Pullo. Why not get fancier digs?"

"I don't know what you're talking about; I'm just a manager here."

"I hear you, deny, deny, deny. See you around, boys."

Once they were out on the street and back in their car, Justina laughed. "I know I'm Italian and it might sound biased, but I still say that the Giacconi Family will win the war."

"Hell, I'm a distant relation to Vladimir Lenin and I know that Krupin will lose. The spoiled little punk won't know what hit him either."

"That Sammy kid was cute, but I don't like long hair on men. I also like my men more mature," Justina said, then she stared at her partner.

Tamir wondered if there was a message behind her words, but no, he was too old for Justina.

"Why don't we go have lunch?" he said.

"Italian?"

Tamir laughed. "I sure as hell don't want any borscht."

24

VIOLATED

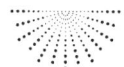

Tanner woke with a start, as an arm fell across his throat.

As he blinked against the daylight filtering in past the edge of the drapes, he looked down and saw that Sara had rolled over in her sleep and had placed her left arm over him. When she moved again, her arm lowered and was now laying on his bare chest, while her face was just inches from his own.

He stared down along her body. She was wearing a set of silk pajamas that did little to hide her curves, while the front of her shirt was parted enough to allow him a view of the tops of her breasts.

Sara Blake had been a target of his gun, had been an enemy, and without doubt, an enormous pain in the ass, but Tanner never once lost sight of the fact that she was a beautiful woman. He envied any man who had found his way into her bed.

He then realized that he was one of those men, since he was lying in her bed at that very moment. The thought made him let out a laugh. Sara stirred at the sound, but instead of waking, she snuggled closer and buried her face in his neck, as her breasts pressed against his arm.

"Blake?"

Sara mumbled in her sleep.

"Blake!"

Her eyes opened, and her hand caressed his chest, as she was still halfway in and out of sleep. She then lifted her head up, and as she saw Tanner smiling at her, she scurried back over to her side of the bed with an embarrassed expression on her face.

"Sorry. I guess I moved around in my sleep."

Tanner grabbed the blanket and pulled it up to his chin.

"You were touching me, Blake. I feel so violated."

Sara stared at him for a moment, then she laughed out loud.

"You have a good sense of humor, Tanner; that's the last thing I expected from you."

"You have your moments as well, and it looks like the rebels ignored us last night."

Tanner went to the bathroom to relieve his bladder and brush his teeth. When he returned, he found Sara sitting up on the edge of the bed and yawning.

"I'm tired; I kept thinking that every little noise was a rebel breaking into the room."

"I don't mind the lack of sleep, but I dread having to play Robert Coleman again."

Sara rose from the bed and stretched. "I'm going to take another shower and wash my hair. Would you please call room service and have them send up coffee and eggs Benedict? I'm hungry this morning."

"You got it."

After grabbing fresh clothes to put on, Sara turned in the threshold to the bathroom and looked back at Tanner.

"Thank you, for not misinterpreting my… what happened in bed. It really was accidental."

"I know that. If anything, you'd be more inclined to strangle me in your sleep than caress me."

Sara shook her head vehemently. "No, I'm done with hate. I just want to get my sister, go home, and try to build a new life. Once this is over, you'll never have to worry about me again. I swear it, although, I guess that you have no reason to trust my word."

"I do trust you. What happened back in New York was driven by paranoia. I don't think you'll make that mistake again."

Sara's eyes saddened. "That mistake cost me too much to learn."

Tanner held up the phone to distract her. He could see that she was about to drift back into despair and feelings of guilt over Johnny Rossetti's death and he wanted to keep that from happening.

"I'll call for the food, and how about some orange juice?"

"Make it pineapple," Sara said, before disappearing into the bathroom.

They were riding down in the elevator with Tanner dreading another day of playacting, when he realized the machine was descending without making a single stop on the lower floors, something that was very unusual in a busy hotel.

He whispered to Sara. "I think something is up."

"We're not stopping."

"Exactly."

Not only did the machine not stop, but it also failed to

open its doors at the lobby level and continued on to the basement.

Tanner and Sara braced themselves as the doors slid open and then they both felt the stinging barbs of a Taser, as they were blasted with enough electricity to drop them to the floor of the elevator car.

Tanner felt himself being lifted by two pairs of strong hands, then he was dropped onto something soft.

He had been deposited into a laundry cart and assumed that Sara was experiencing the same. He stifled his instinct to fight back as a damp rag was pressed over his nose and mouth. His last conscious thought was recognition that he was being rolled onto a truck and then the feeling of movement, as the truck was placed in gear.

As much as he despised not being in control, he was thankful the rebels had struck early, because it saved him the trouble of having to pretend to be bigmouth Robert Coleman again. That was worth a Taser blast any day.

25
THE RIGHT BOY

Jennifer watched as rebels returned from their search of the jungle. She could tell by their faces that they had once again failed to find Jake.

She and the other hostages were down at the edge of a stream, but their pairings had been separated, so that she and Melissa were seated several feet away from Juan Rio and Dr. Washburn.

When Melissa saw the smile on Jennifer's face, she asked her what had caused it.

Jennifer leaned in and whispered to her. "The man that's been attacking them, he's my boyfriend. His name is Jake Garner and he's an FBI agent."

Melissa almost squealed in excitement, but she fought the impulse. "Oh my God, are you serious? Oh, that's so romantic."

"It's incredibly dangerous is what it is. I knew he was here, because he had changed his plans at the last second and took a later flight to join me, but I assumed that he had either flown back home or was waiting at the resort in Telunas for news."

Melissa's eyes shone bright. "But he's here and he's trying to rescue you. He must be so brave, and he must really love you."

Jennifer smiled. "I love him too, even if we haven't been together very long."

"You must have started as friends."

"We did, how did you know?"

"Just a guess, and I have a friend back home that I wish was more than a friend."

"What's his name?"

"Drake Harper and even Daddy likes him… and I want him to be my first."

Jennifer was surprised by that last statement. "You're still a virgin?"

Melissa nodded. "I've been waiting for the right boy, and now, I may never live long enough to be with him."

Jennifer hugged the girl. "Don't think that way. We'll be rescued, and you'll live a long life."

"Yeah, you're right, and it will be your Jake who rescues us."

Jennifer smiled, but her heart was sick with worry for Jake, as she watched a new patrol go off to search for him.

26

TEMPTATION

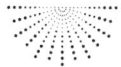

BACK IN NEW YORK CITY THE SKY WAS GROWING DARK AS a meeting was ending inside the Cabaret Strip Club. New Don of the Giacconi Family, Joe Pullo, finished discussing business with his Capos.

Sophia was at the club, sitting at the bar with Laurel, as the two women had surprised themselves by becoming friends. Although, as a woman, Sophia could never be considered a made member of her family, she was still acting as a liaison between the Calvino Crime Family and the Giacconi Family.

As the other men left the club, Sammy Giacconi leaned on the bar and stared down its length at Sophia.

"You like Sophia, don't ya?"

Sammy turned around and saw Merle and Earl smiling at him. It was Merle who had spoken. Sammy grinned at him.

"Hell yeah, I like her, and she's so beautiful she takes my breath away."

"That's Tanner's girl; do you know who he is?" Earl asked.

Sammy nodded. "Everybody has heard of Tanner, but I've never met him."

"We know that," Merle said. "Because you're still breathin', but you might not be if he catches you starin' at his girl that way."

Sammy frowned. "I'm not scared of Tanner. And besides, it's not like they're married."

Earl shrugged. "It's your funeral."

AT THE OTHER END OF THE BAR, SOPHIA ASKED LAUREL a question.

"Is he still staring at me?"

"Yes, and I think my brothers are teasing him."

"He is a hot one, but hell, I must be ten years older than him."

"And there's Tanner to consider, no?"

"It would do Tanner good to see me with another guy, maybe then he wouldn't take me for granted."

"Does he do that?"

"Yeah, but it's my fault, I got a thing for him and he knows it."

"If you're looking for a commitment, don't look to Tanner. It frightens him."

"And if it didn't, then you two would be together, right?"

"I think so, but the chance for that to happen is in the past; now Joe is the only man I want to be with."

Sophia saw movement from the corner of her eye and smiled. "Here he comes."

Sammy said hello to Laurel, then spoke to Sophia. "Why don't you and I go have dinner? And then you can tell me all about yourself."

"Maybe I'm not hungry, did you think of that?"

Laurel stood up. "I have to see Joe about something. So long you two."

Sophia sent her a mock look of annoyance and watched as Sammy took Laurel's empty seat.

"So, what will it be? Italian? Thai? Or maybe you're into sushi?"

Sophia scowled at Sammy. "If you're looking for an easy lay, kid, you got the wrong woman. And I emphasize the word woman."

"You're not that much older than me, and I'm not a kid."

Sophia sighed as she tilted her head slightly. "I actually could go for some grilled sea bass."

Sammy jumped to his feet. "I'm ready when you are. And this is just dinner and conversation, okay?"

"Okay."

As they headed for the door, Sammy looked back at Merle and Earl and sent them a wink.

Vance watched Sammy and Sophia leave the club from a hidden observation post on a nearby rooftop and reconsidered his plans to shoot Joe Pullo when he exited the strip club.

He had seen the group of men leave the club earlier and realized it was being used for meetings of the Giacconi Family's hierarchy.

Vance smiled to himself. *Why kill one man when you can kill twenty?*

Vance eased away from the observation post and made his way back to his vehicle with plans to return. And the next time, he wouldn't be alone.

27

DESPERATION AND DESPAIR

When Tanner came to, he realized he was hanging suspended while also moving backwards, and that there was burning pain in his wrists and ankles.

As he moved his head up to look around, he saw that he was lashed to a pole and that two rebels were toting him along. Sara was also being carried, but by the way her head lolled, Tanner assumed that she had yet to awaken.

When one of the men realized he was conscious, they stopped their procession and lowered them to the ground in a small clearing, slid the poles free, and left them with their wrists and ankles bound together by rope.

Tanner called to Sara, hoping to stir her to consciousness. "Blake, wake up!"

Tanner's head snapped back as one of the rebels backhanded him. He glared up at the man and saw the face of a thug looking back at him, as the man shouted for him to be quiet.

The four men huddled together, and Tanner realized that he could understand almost every word but was disturbed by the topic of their conversation. They were deciding who would rape Sara first.

That simple fact told Tanner that these weren't the religious extremists that were behind the assassination and quest for independence, but rather, opportunists looking to get rich by collecting ransoms. Still, the men might know how to reach the rebel camp, since they appeared to be headed toward their own jungle hideout. Tanner needed to keep one alive to interrogate.

There was good news as well, since he spotted no guns, although each man was armed with a machete.

Sara let out a moan as she awakened, and Tanner saw the men seemed pleased by it. They likely enjoyed the act of rape more when the woman was aware and screaming in terror.

"Blake, wake up! You've got trouble coming. These men want to hurt you."

Sara shook her head as her eyes opened wide. "What's going on?"

"They want to rape you, all of them."

"Oh God!"

"Listen to me. I'll stop them, but it might take—"

Tanner was interrupted as a booted foot kicked him on the chin. As he lay in the dirt recovering from the blow, he realized that the boot was one of his and that the man who kicked him had confiscated them for his own use.

Sara screamed as the other three men grabbed at her and began ripping her dress open. She fought them as best she could, but Tanner knew it was a losing battle.

He made it to his bound feet and wobbled atop the uneven ground, then he made a promise to the man guarding him.

"You're all going to die."

The man didn't understand the words, but took their meaning, and his laughter mixed with Sara's screams.

Jennifer's mood darkened in direct proportion to the width of the smile spreading on Firman's face. The leader of their rebel captors had received good news from a man who had rushed back from patrol to deliver it.

When Jennifer saw that Dr. Washburn looked crestfallen, she knew he had overheard at least part of Firman's conversation, and that it was bad news. She nudged Melissa, who was still attached to her, to move toward the doctor and Juan Rio, then she asked Washburn what he knew.

"They have the man who's been stalking them trapped a mile or two from here and think it's just a matter of time until they capture him."

Jennifer was saddened by the news, but at least it meant that she would be seeing Jake soon. When she wondered aloud how soon he would be joining them, Juan shook his head.

"The doc here says that Firman gave the rebel orders to tell the other men to capture the bloke alive, but only so they could torture him for information… and then kill him. After that, they're to stand watch along the trail for a day in case anyone else shows. It also sounds like we'll be on the march again."

Jennifer collapsed in tears, as Melissa hugged her.

Washburn patted her on the shoulder. "Yes, it is upsetting. I think that man may have been our last hope."

"It's worse than that," Melissa said. "That man is Jennifer's boyfriend; he was trying to rescue her."

"Oh no," Washburn sighed.

Jennifer's grieving was cut short, as she and the other prisoners were ordered to get to their feet and start moving north again. Although she tried to fight it, a steady stream of tears fell down Jennifer's cheeks.

28

UP CLOSE AND PERSONAL

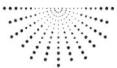

TANNER CURSED AT THE MAN GUARDING HIM IN A LANGUAGE the thug understood and saw anger well up in the kidnapper's dark eyes.

After doubling down on the invectives, he sent a gob of spit that landed on the man's face. It got the reaction he was hoping for, as the man raised his machete to strike.

Tanner did his best to judge the angle of the blow as he leaned back while thrusting his bound wrists upwards toward the blade. He was attempting to meet the blade's sharp edge just as it returned from reaching the apex of the swing. If he placed his hands in the wrong position, he could easily lose a finger or bleed to death from a severed artery or vein.

The blade cut through the bonds and took a chunk out of the pad of skin beneath Tanner's right thumb. He ignored the pain, and even the impulse to look at the wound, as he focused his attention on gaining possession of the machete.

While the blade was still at the bottom of its arc, Tanner bent his knees, leapt up, and sent his bound feet into the man's face. The thug tumbled backwards to the ground, while Tanner, who was also flat on his back, rolled over and trapped the arm still holding the machete. He then delivered an elbow strike against the man's throat.

As the man made a gurgled cry of pain, the men attempting to rape Sara turned their heads and saw what was going on.

One of the men was lying atop of Sara, as he had just torn away her underwear. With her hands still bound together and her feet trapped, Sara used another weapon at her disposal, her mouth. She brought her head up, clamped her teeth over the man's ear, and bit the damn thing off.

Meanwhile, Tanner had gotten his hands on the first man's machete and raised it as if to cut the bindings on his ankles.

The move was just a feint, and as two of the men left Sara and ran toward him, he fell on his back, made a wide swooping motion with the machete, and placed vicious cuts on the ankles of the men running toward him.

Both men stumbled, and as they moved past him, Tanner caught them from behind with a slash to their thighs. He severed the hamstrings of one man, while slicing open the femoral artery of the other man, who had just turned back around.

As he cut through the rope on his ankles, Tanner watched them moan in agony and whimper in fear for their lives. He then left them to finish off the last man.

He found that he was hardly needed. After she had bitten off her attacker's ear, Sara had kneed the man in the groin, gained control of his machete, and was holding it by its handle, after having embedded the first six inches of it into the man's abdomen.

The would-be rapist was staring down at the

protruding blade with wide unbelieving eyes, as Tanner walked over and sliced through Sara's bonds.

He kept his eyes to the task, as her body was exposed beneath her torn garments. As he freed her, he asked if she was all right.

"I'll be fine… thanks to you."

He whispered in her ear. "Keep him alive for now; we may need him to gain information."

Sara answered him with a slight nod and Tanner went to finish off the other men, but before he left, he removed his shirt and draped it around Sara's shoulders.

The man he had hit in the throat with his elbow was already dead. The thug's tanned face was still bright red from the lack of oxygen that was the cause of his demise.

The man with the cut hamstrings was writhing in the dirt. Tanner left him to follow the trail of red the man with the severed artery had left behind. He didn't have to go far, and found the dead man lying beside a tree.

He gathered up the machetes, checked the men for anything of use and retrieved his stolen boots. Afterwards, he dragged the man with the injured hamstrings closer to Sara and left him beside the man with the severe stomach wound.

Both men forgot their pain for a moment, as shock filled their eyes when they realized that Tanner spoke their language, even though he did so badly and with a horrible accent.

Sara stood beside Tanner and went to work wrapping cloth around the wound on his right palm, which was dripping blood. She had covered herself as best she could; however, Tanner's shirt fell to just above her knees. She was naked beneath it, as her undergarments had all been ripped or cut away.

"What did you say to them?" she asked.

"I told them that the first one to give me directions to the rebel camp wouldn't be harmed again."

The man with the damaged legs pushed back his pain and let loose a string of vitriol at Tanner, with an added insult thrown in toward Sara.

Tanner made a casual movement with the machete and sliced open the man's chest, bisecting the nipples and causing blood to flow freely.

Sara turned away from the disturbing wound but heard the man with one ear begin to jabber away, as he gave Tanner directions to the rebel camp.

Tanner went back and forth with the man as he attempted to understand him. When he was certain that he understood where the camp was located, he told Sara it was time to move on.

Sara pointed down at the two men, both of whom were moaning from their injuries. "What about them?"

"They'll both be dead of blood loss by nightfall, or possibly get attacked and devoured by animals."

"It's better than they deserve."

Tanner stopped at the body of the man who had died by asphyxiation and began stripping him of his clothes, while he spoke to Sara.

"If I cut the bottoms off his pants we can use some of the rope to make a belt for you, otherwise, your legs will be eaten by mosquitoes."

A minute later, and Sara had a pair of baggy pants to go with Tanner's shirt, while he claimed the man's tunic for himself.

Sara looked around at the dead and dying men, then she gripped Tanner's good hand in a show of gratitude.

"I don't want to think about what would have happened to me if you were anyone else."

Tanner gestured back toward the man she had

wounded. "I had help. And did you spit the ear out or swallow it?"

Sara's eyes twinkled with mischief. "Spit or swallow? Don't you think that's a little personal?"

And as she walked away laughing, Tanner cleared his throat, then jogged to catch up to her.

29

THE ROOKIE

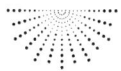

Jake Garner came to the edge of the cliff and realized that he was trapped.

The drop below looked to be about sixty feet and the stream at the bottom was too shallow to jump into without breaking a leg, or worse, his neck.

The distinct sounds of at least two men were drawing closer, one from each side. After turning and running back the way he had come, Jake was felled by a rifle butt to the side of his head. As he lay on his back and the world around him began to fade away, Jake silently cursed himself for failing Jennifer, and wondered if he would ever wake again.

In New York City, Sophia laughed aloud once more as Sammy told her one of his many stories.

Sammy had talked her into going for a ride in a horse-drawn Hansom cab, after Sophia scoffed and said they were strictly for tourists. Afterwards, she admitted that she loved the experience and would do it again.

After the cab ride, they took a booth inside a bar and Sammy listened as Sophia talked about her father and brother. He later mentioned that he had met Jackie Verona once when he was a child, and his grandfather, Sam, was still running the Family.

Before Sammy could launch into another tale, Sophia reached across and took his hand.

"I'm having a good time, thanks. I needed to laugh; it's been a rough week."

"Are you worried about Tanner?"

"A little, but there's no one tougher."

"That's what Uncle Joe says too."

"He's not really your uncle, is he?"

"No, but he's looked out for me ever since my father died in the last war we had with the Russians, and my grandfather thought of him as a son."

SAMMY INSISTED ON SEEING SOPHIA ALL THE WAY HOME TO Staten Island, and as they stood outside her door, she gave him a peck on the cheek.

"I don't know if you expected more, but I am kind of seeing someone."

"You mean Tanner?"

"Yeah."

Sammy stared into her eyes. "If that doesn't work out for you; I want you to know that I'm interested."

"You don't think I'm too old for you?"

"Hell no, and I'm not too young for you. So what do you say, can I at least live on hope?"

Sophia giggled. "Do you know baseball?"

"Of course, and I'm a die-hard Yankees fan."

"Then you'll know what I mean when I say you can stand in the on-deck circle."

"Awesome, and if you ever let me up to bat, I plan to make rookie of the year."

Sophia laughed again. "Goodnight, Sammy, I had fun."

"Goodnight, Sophia."

Sophia gave Sammy a smile, then she unlocked her door and went inside.

Sammy held it in until he believed he was far enough away that Sophia wouldn't hear it, and then he let out a shout of glee.

Inside the house, Sophia had been leaning back against her door. When she heard Sammy's boyish howl of joy, she shook her head and laughed once again.

30

YOU'RE WITH HIM?

Sara surprised Tanner by keeping pace with him, as he alternately ran and then stopped to listen for any sound that would tell them they were not alone.

Listening to discern the movement of humans was not an easy task. The jungle was alive with sounds. While most of it came from the numerous birds that chittered about, there was often the murmur of running water, the rustle of movement made by small mammals, and the occasional squeal from above, as long-tailed monkeys climbed and played among the tree branches.

Swarms of gnats were encountered often, as mosquitoes buzzed and bit, and when Sara leaned against the wrong tree, Tanner informed her that dozens of small red spiders had crawled onto her. She cringed while he swatted the insects off her back.

The only weapons they carried were the machetes taken from the men who abducted them. If they ran into anyone with a gun they would be in trouble.

When the faint cry of pain came from their left, it was

Sara who heard it, but after they moved toward the source, Tanner heard it as well.

Afterwards, they agreed the wailing sounded as if it were coming from a man and they moved stealthily through the trees to find the origin of the sound. The task became difficult when the cries of pain ceased for a time, but when another one came again and was intoned with pure agony, they headed directly toward the sound and found the source of it nearly a mile away.

When Jake Garner regained consciousness, it came slowly, but when the first of his fingernails was pried up with the tip of a knife and then yanked off, he came fully awake in an agonizing instant.

He was strung up between two trees with the toes of his bare feet just able to touch the ground beneath him, and while one man gripped his fingers, another tore off his nails, and a third man looked on with a happy expression, while laughing like a child.

The torture ceased for a time, as one of the men questioned him by using bad English. Jake stalled and lied as well as he was able, but eventually the torture resumed.

The agony was cumulative, and as the fourth nail was ripped from his left hand, he felt as if he were about to pass out again. However, Jake staved off the darkness as hope dawned. The man who'd been about to pry up his thumbnail suddenly went rigid with shock, as the bloody tip of a machete poked out of his throat.

Jake filled with hope, only to have it dashed when he saw that the man who killed his tormentor was Tanner.

I must be hallucinating, Garner thought, and then assumed it confirmed, because next, he spotted Sara Blake fighting beside Tanner. If they were within reach of each other while brandishing machetes they would be using them on one another.

Sara dispatched the man who had found Garner's pain humorous by slicing him open at the middle. As the rebel lay in the dirt dying, his own cries of agony left him joyless.

After plunging his blade through the torturer's neck, Tanner withdrew it and shoved it past the ribs of the man who had been holding Jake's hand in place. That punctured the man's heart and left him to drop like a stone.

Tanner slapped Jake lightly on the cheek to revive him, then issued a command. "Hold still!"

Two quick chops with a machete and Garner was freed from his bonds. He collapsed to his knees, with Sara kneeling beside him.

"Is this real?"

Sara smiled. "Yes, and you're safe now."

As Sara gathered up the rifle and lone revolver that belonged to the men they'd slain, Tanner helped Garner walk to a stream that was fifty yards away. After they'd all drank their fill of water, Garner gingerly washed his damaged hand in the stream.

When they were all seated on the ground, Sara looked over Garner's wounds and Tanner inspected the rifle and gun. Both were fully loaded and appeared to be in firing condition. Tanner kept the rifle, but he passed the gun to Sara.

Jake looked first at Tanner, and then at Sara. "You two working together has got to be one hell of a story, but right now I'm more concerned about Jennifer. Please tell me there's more help on the way?"

"There is," Tanner said. "Conrad Burke is waiting for us to signal him, and then he'll send in a group of men."

Jake made a grim face at that news. "I came across the bodies of the last men he sent. I hope he has better luck this time. And Tanner, Sara, thank you. If you hadn't come along I'd be dead."

Tanner stood. "Are you good to travel?"

"I am, but my left hand may be almost useless for a while."

"Were they torturing you for fun, or did they want information?"

"It was both, but the man who had been holding my wrist spoke a little English. He asked me if I was 'Here on my lonesome,' I lied and said that I wasn't, but they saw through it."

"It's a good thing they did," Sara said. "Otherwise, they might have searched and come across us."

Jake smiled. "I've seen her, Sara. I saw Jennifer and she seemed to be all right. There are also five other hostages, two women and three men."

"Did she see you?"

Jake's smile turned to a frown. "I think she saw me, but by now she probably believes I'm dead."

The only thing that slowed Jennifer's tears was the frantic pace Firman insisted the party keep to, as they finally neared the rebel camp.

George and Reba were having a difficult time keeping up, and when Jennifer looked back at George, she feared that the red-faced man was on the verge of having a heart attack.

Another hour passed, an hour in which even the young rebels began to appear fatigued, and at last, Firman directed them toward a riverbank where they would rest and eat.

Juan wiped at his brow and pulled at the sweat-drenched shirt that clung to his skin.

"My wife has been after me to lose ten pounds. No need to now, I must have lost at least that the last few days."

"This is torture," George rasped out, as his wife lay beside him on her back, while still gulping in air. Then everyone looked over at Jennifer and saw the tears in her eyes.

Melissa gave her hand a squeeze. "Those screams we heard might have come from someone else."

Jennifer wiped at her eyes. "It was Jake. They tortured him and now he's probably dead because he tried to help me."

They were given food as the sun was fading from sight. It consisted of raw fish and gummy rice. Dr. Washburn insisted that Jennifer eat, but she declined, knowing that it would never stay down.

She was deep in despair, unaware that not only was Jake alive, but that he had gained two very capable allies.

31

NOBODY'S PERFECT

Tanner fashioned a lean-to between two trees, after gathering branches and hacking at smaller trees with one of the machetes.

Sara had helped him, while an exhausted Jake rested. By nightfall, they were beneath the flimsy shelter and eating cured meat, which Tanner had taken from the pack of one of the men he killed earlier.

When Sara asked Tanner what sort of meat the jerky was made from, he told her to keep eating and to try not to think about it.

When Jake awoke, he and Sara took the first watch. While Tanner slept, Sara filled Jake in on what had happened to her over the last few days, while speaking in whispers.

When she told him about Johnny Rossetti, he placed an arm around her shoulders.

"I'm sorry, Sara. I know that he meant something to you."

"I loved him, Jake, and it's my fault that he's dead."

Jake glanced over at the lean-to, where Tanner slept.

"His presence here tells me how much you've changed, but why is he here?"

"I could have killed him, and I didn't, on the condition that he help me find and rescue Jenny."

"So, he's here against his will?"

Sara's face scrunched up as she considered the question. "No, despite our agreement, he's here of his own free will, and I might be dead if he weren't helping me."

"Does that have anything to do with those rags you're wearing?"

"These pants, yes, four men tried to rape me, but Tanner stopped them. He really is remarkable, and so are you. I'm so sorry that I doubted your feelings for Jenny."

"I love her, I mean I must. My only thought is to find her and hold on to her forever."

AS THE FIRST RAYS OF SUNLIGHT LIT THE JUNGLE, TANNER reached into the lean-to and shook Sara's shoulder.

"We should get an early start."

Sara yawned. "Oh, I ache all over and it feels like I barely slept."

"If our information is correct, the camp is only a few hours away. Once we reach it, we'll send a message to Burke."

Jake sat up and rubbed a hand over his face. "How are you going to make contact?"

Tanner rolled up a sleeve on the tunic he was wearing and showed Jake the tiny bump on his forearm.

"This is a GPS tracker. When we find Blake's sister, I'll cut it out and destroy it. Then Burke will send a team of men to our last known coordinates."

"I hope his men do a better job this time around."

"I spoke to him about that as his people were putting the GPS chip in my arm," Tanner said. "Burke promised me he would rain down hell upon them this time. From what I overheard when they were putting in the tracker, he's bought an old helicopter for the mission. Once we find the camp, it shouldn't take very long for help to arrive."

Sara walked off toward the stream to wash and prepare for the day. When she was out of sight, Jake grabbed Tanner's arm.

"I don't know why you're doing this, but thank you."

"You're welcome, but Blake and I have a deal. Once her sister is safe, the two of us will be done with each other."

"She explained to me how she got the better of you, by threatening the woman you love. I have to say, I'm surprised to learn that you have a heart."

Tanner sighed. "Nobody's perfect."

32

TRUST ME

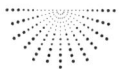

In New York City, Laurel returned from a day at the clinic to find a candlelight dinner waiting for her. After a quick shower and a change of clothes, she joined Joe at her dining room table.

"This is unexpected. What's the occasion?" Laurel said.

Joe wiped his sweaty palms on his pants and moved the napkin that had been hiding the ring box.

Laurel's mouth dropped open in shock and widened still more when Joe opened the box and revealed a huge diamond ring.

"Before you say anything, I just want you to know that I'm aware I'm moving fast here, but after watching Johnny die when he least expected it, I know that life can end at any time. I'll be damned if I'm going to die without at least taking a shot at getting you to marry me. So, what do you say?"

Laurel beamed at him. "Ask me properly."

Joe got down on one knee in front of Laurel and held

up the ring box. "Will you marry me, baby? I love you more than anything."

"Yes. I'll marry you and I love you too. I love you so much."

Joe rose to his feet as Laurel stood, and the two of them kissed and embraced. When Laurel began pulling him toward the stairs, Joe pointed back at the table.

"What about the food?"

"It can wait; I want to be in your arms and know that we'll always be together."

"That sounds like heaven to me," Joe said, and he swooped Laurel up and headed for the bedroom.

IN ANOTHER PART OF THE CITY, OTHER PLANS WERE BEING made, plans that involved causing Joe Pullo's death. Vance was in Michael Krupin's office along with the young leader of the Russian mob, who was seated behind his desk. Fedor was also present, as Vance told them his latest plan to gain the upper hand in the war.

"How sure are you that they'll meet again at that club?"

"Very sure. I followed one of the men who had attended the meeting and tortured him. The club is closed due to Rossetti's death and the fact that Pullo is fearful that we might have attacked it while it was full of customers."

Krupin grimaced at the very thought. "That's the last thing I would do. I have enough scrutiny on me now after the slaughter the other day. Killing civilians would really bring down the hammer."

"In any event, Pullo is using the place as a headquarters. When he holds his next meeting, it will be a golden opportunity to wipe out the Giacconi's top men, Pullo included."

"How many men will you need?" Krupin asked.

"Four men. And I'll also want Fedor with me."

Fedor had been sitting on a love seat at the right side of the room, but he stood and walked over to Vance.

"Why do you want me there?"

"I'll need someone who is good with a rifle and I hear that you're a decent shot."

"I'm the best there is, and I understand that you're a marksman too, but I guess you'll need me to cover one of the exits from the club, no?"

"Exactly, although I doubt anyone will make it out alive."

Fedor stared at Vance for several seconds, then he looked over at Krupin. "I have to say, it is a sound plan and I see little risk to our men."

"Our men?" Krupin said, while raising one eyebrow.

"As they say here, a figure of speech, but I too keep the men's concern in my mind, especially after having lost so many of them recently."

Krupin made a sour face at those words and drummed his fingers on the desktop as he thought things over.

The street sounds of a city drifted up from outside the second story windows and they could hear someone shouting for a taxi to stop. The constant hum of traffic only paused when an equal stream of pedestrians needed to cross, as they continued along their seemingly endless journeys.

After nearly a minute had passed, Krupin nodded once at Vance. "We'll do it, but Rurik, if this plan fails you won't get any more chances, understood?"

Vance smiled. Yes, he understood, and after killing

Pullo, he planned to kill Krupin as well and then take control of his empire.

"Everything will work out, Michael, trust me."

33

LISTEN AND LEARN

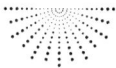

Jennifer gazed down a steep drop at the small valley below and saw scores of men moving about.

There was an actual building, although it appeared to be prefabricated, along with camouflage-colored tents, which were lined up in neat rows, while a structure that resembled a giant birdcage hung from a tree branch, with figures lying inside it.

It was the cage where the rebels held their hostages and it was about to become Jennifer's new home.

Juan Rio had been gazing up at the latticework of pond fronds, rope, and camouflage material that had been rigged between the trees surrounding the camp, placing most of it in the shade, while also obscuring the rebel base from satellite surveillance.

"I bet this place is hard to find," Juan said.

There were men stationed along the trail here. They had encountered them as they walked the last mile of their trek.

Salt air wafted on the breeze and Jennifer and the other hostages agreed that they were close to the Indian

Ocean, and that the base must receive most of its supplies by sea.

Firman issued a set of orders to his men and the hostages began the short hike into the valley, while wondering if it would become a valley of death.

~

NOT FAR AWAY, TANNER RETURNED FROM SCOUTING AHEAD and informed Sara that there were men guarding the trail.

"That's a good sign, isn't it? It must mean we're growing closer to where the camp is."

"That's true, but it also means that our odds of being discovered are greater. We can't use the guns, or we'll alert the camp that we're nearby."

"We'll have to sneak up on the guards and kill them by hand," Jake said, and Tanner nodded in agreement.

"How many are there?" Sara asked.

"I came across four, two pairs of two, but they were scattered over a long stretch of the trail. Once we kill them, it's just a matter of time until they're missed, or until they change the guards. I suggest we wait and watch before making a move."

Sara shifted from foot to foot as she shook her head in disagreement. "I don't want to wait. God only knows what Jenny is going through."

"Tanner is right," Jake said. "We should wait and gain intel. That way, we can kill the guards right after they change shifts and allow ourselves the maximum amount of time to get in and out."

Sara paced for a moment before speaking. "Okay, as much as I hate to wait another second, I see that you're right."

"There's something else," Tanner said. "I think these

are only the first few guards, there are probably more of them closer to camp."

Sara studied his face. "You have a plan to deal with them?"

"Yes, I'll move ahead alone until I reach the camp. After they change the guards, I'll work my way back to you, even as you two are working your way toward me."

"By working, you mean killing, right, hit man?" Jake said.

"That's right, Special Agent Garner and I'll be killing in a cause to free your woman."

Jake held up a hand as if to say he was sorry. "I apologize, Tanner. I don't think we'd have a chance without your help."

"You may not have one with me, but I'll do my best to help you."

Sara placed a hand on his arm. "We'll watch and wait, and after they change the guards, we'll meet you in the middle."

"Kill as quietly as you can," Tanner said, then he moved into the trees on his left and disappeared.

"Your attitude toward him has certainly changed," Jake said.

Sara gazed at the spot where Tanner disappeared. "I've come to see that sometimes killing is necessary, and not just under the law or for self-defense. And there's no one better at killing than Tanner."

"You're just using him? And what happens when we get Jennifer back, will you try to kill him?"

"No. Jake, I really have made peace with the man, and I don't have it in me to hate anymore. I can't even bring myself to hate the men who took Jenny. I just want her back and then I'll somehow get on with my life."

"It's good to hear you talk that way, and if he helps us

get Jennifer back, Tanner has earned a pass on anything as far as I'm concerned. Now come on, let's get into position."

Sara and Jake moved on, as behind them and hidden from view, Tanner moved on as well. Sara Blake appeared to be telling the truth this time and Tanner was glad.

After the events of the last few days, it would have hurt him to kill her, and that wasn't something he could say about many people.

Tanner moved toward the camp, machete in hand, prepared to do what he did best, as death walked by his side.

34
WELCOME TO HELL

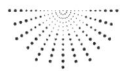

Firman got down on his knees and bowed before his superior, a man in his sixties who was wearing robes and sandals and had a mane of white hair.

The man gestured for Firman to rise, and when he looked over at the hostages he made a face of disgust, as if the very sight of the westerners sickened him.

His name was Raden Soekemi, but he was respectfully referred to as Gus Soe by his subordinates, a name that was uttered only with reverence and respect.

Raden Soekemi was born the son of a wealthy banker in Jakarta and was raised learning the language of money. The intricacies of money handling such as fractional-reserve banking and hypothecation filled him with boredom, and as a young man, he drifted into the arena of law.

The rich had power, of that there was no doubt, but the power of the law and the deference given toward lawyers drew him in and he became one of them.

And as he had learned the secret language and ways of finance at his father's knee, Raden also learned the ways and language of the law from his professors and went on to practice it for years.

Having found success as a lawyer, Raden then turned his attention toward becoming a lawmaker, a policy baron, and he went on to learn yet another language and set of customs, the terminology and rules of politics.

With his power and esteem at a height far beyond any his father had ever attained, Raden became fascinated by the sway that the religious leaders held over the people. Once again, he learned new ways and customs as he reinvented himself, then surprised himself and became a true believer of his religion, and later, grew militant in his beliefs.

But Raden, who was now the venerable Gus Soe, sought to climb even higher by becoming the leader of a separatist movement, whose true goal was to take power. It was he who had ordered the assassination of President Urray, his guiding hand behind the kidnappings, and his holy wisdom would guide his adopted country of Guambi. It was his belief that someday he would be acknowledged as the country's leader.

RADEN SMILED AT FIRMAN. THE MAN WAS AS FANATICAL AS he and was soon to be named his second in the cause. Firman had proven himself worthy, by not only overseeing the assassination of the president, but Firman had also delivered the valuable hostages, as he had promised.

Raden watched as one of his aides took pictures of the captives, photographs that would be sent to their families as proof of life. It was the only proof that they would ever receive.

With the photos taken, the hostages became worthless,

although Raden would release one or two of them as incentive for the other families to pay.

When he spotted Jennifer, he eyed her with contempt, for she reminded him of a woman whom he had known in his youth. The woman had been a slut who would have sex with anyone for as little as a free meal, but the witch had always made snide comments about the size of his manhood.

Raden had killed that woman, quite by accident while in a fit of rage, and had disposed of her corpse with no more thought than he would have given a dead rat.

He had desired her body, longed to caress her blonde hair, and now the sight of that same color on Jennifer brought back the feelings of inadequacy the wanton woman of his youth had made him feel so long ago. It was not a sensation Raden enjoyed.

WITH THE PHOTOS TAKEN, FIRMAN ISSUED ORDERS TO HIS men. Prendy and the other rebels began herding the hostages toward the cage at the other end of the compound, which hung about a foot off the ground.

The odor hit Jennifer before they had even drawn near. It was a foulness of feces, urine, and fetid water joined together, and it was emanating from the hole dug beneath the cage. Worst of all was the stench of rotted flesh, and as they peered down into the pit, two corpses were visible.

Melissa cried as Mrs. Hough gagged, and then the door on the cage was opened. They were all herded up and inside the swaying contraption at the point of machetes.

There were already four prisoners in the cage, all Australian, three men and a woman, who Jennifer thought looked as if they had been there for months. When they told her that they had only been there two days, she briefly wondered what toll the ordeal was taking on her own appearance.

There was a tight weave of rope along the bottom of the cage, save for a corner, where one went to do their business, with zero privacy. The waste would fall into the pit atop the corpses.

"This is bloody inhumane!" Juan shouted. His words rewarded him with a jab in the back from a stick the guards kept on the ground for disciplinary purposes.

Juan winced in pain, then fell and settled on his ass, while rubbing the place where he was struck.

One of the men who had already been there when they arrived looked around at the newcomers and sent them a grim smile.

"Welcome to hell."

~

LATER, WITH MOST OF THE MEN IN THE CAMP INSIDE THE largest tent and eating a meal, the young rebel Prendy paid the cage a visit. He had just collected money from a bet he'd won and could think of no better use for it than to bribe the guards to give him access to the American girl.

At fourteen, Prendy was even younger than he appeared to be. So hard had his short life been, that the demanding trek through the jungle had been a huge improvement over his normal existence. His former days had consisted of scrounging for food in the dumpsters of the resort hotels, avoiding violent gangs, and sleeping on the beach at night.

When Firman first began spouting his beliefs about a God that loved everyone like a father, Prendy thought the man insane. He still did, but by joining up with the skinny man's cause, he had gained a feeling of fellowship and had been given a gun to hold while guarding the hostages.

As he approached the cage, Prendy rubbed his crotch in anticipation. He had only been with one girl and she had been a skinny thing of twelve years without breasts. He longed to touch Melissa's breasts and ached to be inside her, even knowing that if he were caught with her, he would be in huge trouble.

But he had been nice to her, hadn't he? He had even fed her, so he hoped she would give in to his desires and not make him have to hurt her. If she did cry out, he'd have to kill her and move on to the tall one, the one with the golden hair. Prendy grinned while thinking of the tall one's breasts, which were even larger than the girl's.

Maybe he would have them both.

JENNIFER SAW PRENDY APPROACH THE CAGE WITH A grinning face and watched as he passed something to the two men who were standing guard over them. After looking around furtively, the men came over and opened the cage.

Prendy pointed at Melissa. If not for the lecherous glint in the boy's eyes, Jennifer might have thought he was doing her a kindness by removing her from the nightmare that was the cage, even if only for a short time.

"Something's not right here," Juan said, and when Jennifer looked over at Melissa, she saw that the girl was frightened.

One of the guards gestured for Melissa to come out of the cage, but she shook her head as tears began to flow.

Prendy spoke to her in a loud whisper, then he

unsheathed his machete and entered the cage. When Juan stood up, Prendy swung the machete at him and just missed slicing open his face. Then, he grabbed Melissa by the wrist and began pulling her toward the cage opening.

Melissa cried and thrashed about, which made Prendy even angrier and caused the guards to look back toward the mess tent.

One of the guards said something to Prendy and the boy slapped Melissa on the side of her head. The blow stunned her, she fell upon her back, and Prendy reached down and stuck his free hand inside her blouse, to fondle her.

Juan was red with anger and cursing at Prendy with everything he had, even as a guard was repeatedly poking him in the ribs with a stick. Jennifer feared that the father of four girls was about to lose his life in a vain attempt to save Melissa from rape.

A glazed look came over Prendy's face as he felt the girl's breasts. Jennifer knew then that he planned to rape Melissa, and possibly kill her if she regained her senses and resisted.

"Hey!"

Prendy turned toward her with his machete poised to strike, then licked his lips as Jennifer opened her blouse to give Prendy a view of her cleavage.

"Leave her alone and I'll go with you."

Prendy stared at her, then he reached out and touched her short blonde hair.

"That's right, take me and leave her. Don't hurt her."

Prendy jumped down from the cage and gestured for Jennifer to follow, he was so engrossed with the thought of having her that he never noticed Firman leaving the tent and walking his way. No sooner had Jennifer stepped out of the cage to sacrifice herself to save the virginal Melissa,

SUICIDE OR DEATH

when Firman cried out in anger and called back into the tent.

Men flooded from the tent, among them their leader garbed in robes. When Firman reached Prendy, he knocked the boy to the ground with a hard slap across the face and let loose a long string of words in his native language.

The guards were questioned, then escorted away for disciplinary training, which would take the form of a severe beating. Although Jennifer didn't understand a word that was being said, she knew Prendy was in serious trouble for going against the tenets of his religion, by seeking to have sex with her.

When Prendy was dragged off, Jennifer was relieved, but then the white-haired man wearing the robes leaned over and spoke into Firman's ear.

Whatever the man had whispered, it pleased Firman, who turned and pointed at Jennifer, and soon she was being dragged away as well.

"I didn't do anything! I was only trying to protect my friend."

Her words were ignored, if they were even understood. Although she couldn't know it, Jennifer had been marked for death. Death by beheading.

35

KILL AND KILL AGAIN

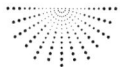

Tanner waited until the guards farthest from the camp came walking along the trail and passed him, before springing into action.

The men were talking to each other about a game of chance and seemed happy to be returning to camp and be done with their workday.

Tanner had gazed down upon the rebel compound from a position not far from the place where Jennifer had stood earlier. He estimated that there were well over a hundred men present between the ones guarding the trail and those in the camp.

He had also taken note of the cage and knew it wouldn't be easy to free anyone from it, as it was in plain sight, with the cliff wall at its back.

The weave of rope and hodgepodge of camouflage materials overhead interested him, and he determined that it had to be destroyed if Burke's men were to have any chance at a successful raid. However, that would come later, after he killed his share of the men guarding the trail.

The first man died easily, because the fool had been

laughing and talking to the second man, who died only an instant later, as Tanner slashed his blade across their necks, thus, opening their throats, and rendering them speechless at the same time he delivered injuries that would kill them.

He watched them thrash on the ground and die by exsanguination, then he listened carefully in case another rebel had drawn near.

There was no need to hide the bodies from view, because the copious amount of blood spilled would speak of their demise anyway, so Tanner moved on.

There were ten men on patrol along the trail. Tanner found his third man looking alert and ready. Tanner stepped into view, took careful aim and hit the man in the face with a stone. He had been aiming for a spot between the man's eyes, but the stone smashed the area high atop the man's forehead and caused him to weave about like a drunk.

Tanner managed to reach him before he recovered, grabbed the rock from the ground, and used it to smash the guard's face repeatedly.

The struggle made little noise. Unfortunately, the fourth man must have been nearby, because Tanner heard someone running along the trail and coming his way.

After switching the machete to his left hand, Tanner ran toward the sound with his blade up and at the ready. As he and the fourth man met at a bend in the trail, Tanner sliced deep along the ribs of a man holding a rifle and watched him crumple onto the dirt.

He walked back to the man, took away the rifle, and delivered a killing stroke with his blade, ending the man's cries of pain, which had been gaining in volume.

He was rounding the bend in the trail when he became aware of the footfalls coming up from behind and had just enough time to duck. A blade whooshed over his head.

When he looked up, he saw a face so damaged that he marveled its owner still had sight.

It was the third guard, the one he had smashed with the rock. The man was speaking gibberish from a mouth whose teeth were freshly broken.

Tanner tripped him with the rifle barrel, even as the man attempted to swing the machete, then he finished the job of killing the man by thrusting a blade into his heart.

Guards five and six suffered from the belief that, being the guards in the middle, they would have sufficient time to be alerted if there was any trouble along either end of the trail. They sat with their backs against a tree while smoking and sharpening their blades.

Tanner crawled over to them on the side of the tree that was directly behind them, and with a machete in each hand, he reached around and sliced open their throats. One man died almost instantly, as the blade had bitten deep. The other man managed to stand and take several steps before falling face-first. He died after suffering a spasm.

Tanner was hidden behind the same tree when he saw Sara and Garner moving along the edge of the trail while keeping to the shadows. He stepped out, raised his hand to grab their attention and saw that their work had left them as bloody as had his own. He also noticed that Jake looked sickened by the violence.

"If I never have to kill with a blade again, it will be too soon," Sara said.

"It does get messy, and personal," Tanner agreed.

After they took a quick stop at a stream to wash off what blood they could, he led them to the view that overlooked the camp.

Sara cried as she took in the cage. "They're keeping her like an animal."

Jake pointed up at the web of camouflage. "That's going to be a problem for the helicopter."

"I can deal with that," Tanner said, "and when I do, all hell will break loose."

When he finished speaking, he dug a fingernail into the skin of his opposite arm and freed the tiny GPS tracker that had been placed there, causing a small trickle of blood to flow. He held the device up.

"Once I destroy this, Burke's people will be on their way here, so why don't we make a plan first?"

"Fine," Sara said. "How will you handle that camouflage tarp above us?"

Tanner removed a lighter and a pack of matches that he had found near the bodies of the two guards that had been smoking.

"I'll set fire to it, which will cause chaos and alert the troops of trouble."

"Won't that endanger Jenny and the other hostages?" Sara said.

"It's a possibility, which is why we'll be freeing them when the fire reaches its peak."

Jake blew out a long breath. "That sounds like suicide."

"Not for you two, because you'll be up here with those rifles and killing any guard that gets in the way."

Sara's face scrunched up in confusion. "How are you going to start the fire and get down there before it burns out of control?"

"I'll manage, trust me."

Sara stared into Tanner's eyes. "I do trust you; I'm trusting you with my sister's life."

"I'll find her, and I'll get her to safety, but while I'm doing that you two will be on your own."

"I told you before we started that getting Jenny to

safety was your only job; Jake and I will take care of ourselves."

"Fine, but for this to work, you both have to be good shots with a rifle. Are you?"

"I'm better than decent, given the range," Sara said. "And if I'm not mistaken, Jake has won contests."

Jake shook his head. "I came in second two years in a row, but yes, I can shoot."

"What about the bad hand?"

"It hurts like hell, but it's good enough to grip the rifle."

"All right, and make every shot count, there's not much ammo."

Tanner placed the GPS chip on the ground and smashed it with a rock. He looked up. "The countdown has begun."

36

GERONIMO!

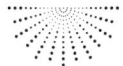

Many of the tall trees in the area had few branches on the lower section of their trunks. Tanner climbed up one of them by using two machetes as if they were claws, and then moved over to where a corner of the huge camouflage net was fastened with thick rope.

His hands were on fire with pain, as the web of flesh on one had been previously wounded by gunfire, while the other had a chunk removed from its palm by the descending blade of a machete, just a day earlier.

No stranger to pain, Tanner pushed it aside and put his mind to the task at hand, freeing Jennifer Blake.

Tanner wasn't certain of just what it was that Burke had planned but assumed that the man would send as large a force as he could gather to wipe out the rebels. What that would cost the man in terms of new government scrutiny and more hearings concerning his company was anyone's guess. Burke wanted his daughter back as much as Sara wanted her sister returned safely. And even in a third-world nation like Guambi, Burke had the connections and resources to get it done.

After giving up on cutting through the many ropes that secured the canopy, Tanner sliced at two of the pieces used, and after shaking them and seeing how long the ropes were, he looked down through a small hole he'd made and estimated the distance to the ground.

An idea occurred to him at that point, one that made him smile. Tanner hoped he wouldn't make a fool of himself when he put it into action, or worse, get himself killed by breaking his neck.

However, he had been a long-range shooter for most of his life and had a keen eye for estimating distances. He was confident he could guess the distance to the ground within a meter.

Tanner crawled out into the center of the tarp while dragging the ropes behind him. When he reached the middle, he broke open the lighter, spilling its flammable fluid atop dry leaves. He then used the book of matches to light it.

The liquid immediately caught fire, the leaves burned, and Tanner waited for his chance to play Tarzan.

Down below on the lip of the cliff overlooking the camp, Sara and Jake lay on their stomachs and gazed down at the sudden flurry of activity taking place.

"What do you think is going on, could they know we're here?" Sara asked.

Jake shook his head. "No, if that were the case, they'd be staring up here. No, it's not us, but something has everyone down there excited."

Sara looked up at the canopy and noticed that there was a black spot at its center, and as she kept looking, she caught the glow of embers.

"Look! He's done it. Tanner has started the fire."

"Good, but that thing is a massive patchwork and may take a while to burn."

Down below, someone let out a cry of joy. When she looked, Sara saw a small figure being dragged from a tent. The figure was male, but not very big, and he was brought out to the rear of the compound with his hands tied behind him, and then forced to his knees.

An instant later, Sara spotted another figure being dragged toward the first, and as soon as she spotted the cropped blonde hair, she knew.

"Jenny, oh my God, that's Jenny."

Jake leaned farther over the rim of the cliff as if another few inches would help him see her better, but he didn't need to see her face clearly, for like Sara, he knew.

Jennifer also had her hands tied behind her back and was driven down to her knees by two rough hands. Moments later, Firman appeared, and as he sharpened a long Katana-style sword, his intent became clear.

"Oh… oh good God, they're going to execute her," Sara said, and both she and Jake knew that the odds had just risen against Jennifer ever seeing another day.

TANNER HAD MOVED AWAY FROM THE FIRE AT THE CENTER of the canopy and had cut another hole to see through. When he spotted Sara's sister being readied for execution, he knew that Burke's men might not reach the area in time to stop it. He also realized the plan he had made with Sara and Jake was now obsolete.

After removing his boots and securing the ropes around his ankles, Tanner hacked at the hole until it was large enough to fit through.

He found himself coughing violently as the wind shifted and blew the smoke of the fire his way, while also feeding it and causing it to grow. Tanner readied himself, while hoping that Sara and Jake wouldn't act too soon, then he prepared to leap literally into the fray.

~

Sara was lining up her shot on Firman when Jake pressed a hand on the barrel of her rifle.

"Don't fire unless there's no other choice. With these rifles, at this distance, we could just as easily hit Jennifer as the man with the sword."

Sara groaned in frustration. "You're right, but we'll soon have to take that risk. Look, he's moving up behind them."

Jake pulled at his hair. "Where are those men of Burke's?"

~

Down below, Firman began speaking as he paced behind Prendy and Jennifer. His fiery speech was a sermon about the evil of promiscuity, the lasciviousness of western women, and the dire consequences of giving in to the appetites of the flesh.

When he stopped and stared at the crowd, most of the men gathered believed he was doing so solely for dramatic effect, but then Firman shifted his feet, raised the sword high, and brought it down against the side of Prendy's neck.

Blood sprayed a dozen feet and the boy's head, now just barely attached, lolled over to settle upon the right shoulder, even as the body was falling forward. Firman reversed the sword's trajectory and sliced between the shoulder and the neck, an act that severed Prendy's head from his body and sent it tumbling off to the side.

Jennifer let out screams of pure terror as she tried to make it to her feet. She was pressed back down upon her knees by two of Firman's men.

Both Sara and Jake had been frozen by the barbarity of the act and numbed with apprehension, but after giving himself a shake, Jake raised his rifle and aimed through the iron sights.

"We've just run out of options; I'll have to take a chance on hitting her."

"Look!" Sara pointed upward, and when Jake followed her gaze, he saw Tanner's head and shoulders emerge from a hole in the canopy.

"What is Tanner doing? Is he getting ready to jump?"

"No, that would be suicide," Sara said, then watched as the fire at the middle of the tarp suddenly expanded, and hot ash began to rain down. When she looked back at the camp, she saw that the men below had taken notice and that many were pointing up.

That's when Tanner jumped out of the hole headfirst and fell over eighty feet. The ropes holding him came to a violent stop, leaving his head less than two feet above the ground, before recoiling. It placed him in the midst of where Jennifer knelt on her knees.

While still upside down and swinging, Tanner took a hack at Firman with one of the two machetes he wielded. The religious fanatic ducked so quickly that he fell backwards and landed on his bony ass, while losing his grip on the sword.

Tanner's blade missed Firman, but bit deep into the venerable white head of the holy one, Gus Soe, who had been standing beside Firman. The blade became lodged inside Gus Soe's holy brain, and sent him to his holy heaven, where he would doubtlessly have to learn the ways and customs of the dead.

Tanner raised his upper body as if he were performing an upside-down sit-up, took a mighty swing at the complex knot that secured the two ropes to his ankles, and cut himself loose. After turning over in midair, he landed on his feet amid a hundred armed men.

Firman, along with the two men who were guarding Jennifer, backed away with her, then disappeared beyond the crowd.

Tanner reached down and grabbed up the bloody sword that had killed Prendy. As the rebels closed in upon him, Tanner turned in a circle, his intense eyes ablaze as he spoke to the men in their own language.

"Who dies first?"

37

CHANGE OF PLANS?

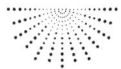

Vance tried to look as if he were taking the news in stride, while also noticing the pleasure Fedor took from delivering it.

The meeting at the Cabaret Strip Club was cancelled and it was Fedor's belief that the reason for the cancellation was because one of the men who attended the last meeting had vanished.

Fedor crossed his legs as he sat on the love seat in Michael Krupin's office, and there was a self-satisfied grin on his face.

"It was stupid of you to kill that man for information when you could have simply bribed one of his soldiers and learned the same things he told you. But now, now Pullo is suspicious and has wisely changed his plans."

"I don't answer to you, Fedor, and there's any number of reasons why Pullo might have postponed the meeting."

Fedor grinned. "You screwed up yet again, admit it, Rurik."

"Fuck you."

Krupin rose from behind his desk and then took a seat

on a corner of it. "Can you fix this? Pullo still needs to die."

Vance sent him a reassuring smile. "Of course, I can fix it. The meeting was just the best of all possible outcomes, but Pullo is still using that club as his office, just as Rossetti did. I'll just use the same plan and soon he'll be history."

Krupin paced about as he thought things over. When he stopped in mid-stride, he pointed at Vance.

"Stick with the plan, but we'll wait a couple of more days. If there's no meeting, then put it into action. And I still want you to take Fedor with you as backup."

Vance nodded in agreement. "Of course, I'll still need another man who is good with a rifle."

"Not good," Fedor said. "I am the best."

Vance shrugged. "That's even better. The club has two exits, while I stand watch over the alley exit, you'll be watching the front, and if by some miracle someone escapes the trap, we shoot them dead."

Fedor grinned. "It sounds like fun."

"Is everything ready? And have you picked out the other men you'll use?" Krupin asked.

"The men are ready; their part in it shouldn't take much more than a minute."

"Who are you using?"

Fedor answered. "It is my Nephew Anton and his boys; they are all good men."

Krupin sighed. "I guess I can look forward to that Fed showing up again."

"No doubt, but you'll have an airtight alibi and there will be no way to trace it back to us."

"Still, I hate that Fed."

"I just hope he brings that little Italian сука with him,"

Fedor said. "I like looking at her. And what do you think, is he doing her, his own partner?"

Krupin spun around and smiled at Fedor. "You've just given me an idea, but one thing at a time, and first, you two will kill Pullo."

Vance patted the holster beneath his jacket. "He's as good as dead."

38

THE MANY, OUTNUMBERED BY THE ONE

BAJA CALIFORNIA, MEXICO, MARCH 1999

Beneath the heat of a desert sun, Tanner Six put his two protégés through their paces as he trained them to one day be the best at what they do, which was killing.

However, there were times that one first had to survive in order to kill, so he also trained them in ways to do that... with varying results.

Romeo stepped out of the contraption that Tanner Six called the Gauntlet and tossed a pair of knives to the ground in frustration.

The Gauntlet was made up of five rotating poles, each with five arms set at various and adjustable heights, and each arm was tipped with red lipstick. The poles were connected by a system of pulleys at their base and would rotate at the spinning of a handle.

The five poles with their five arms represented twenty-five men with knives. If you were marked by one, it would leave a trace in the form of red lipstick, red for blood.

Romeo emerged from the gauntlet covered with over three dozen marks, many that would have been fatal injuries if they were truly the wounds they represented.

"Shit, man, who the hell could face that many men in a knife fight and live?"

"I'm standing here in front of you and I once faced over a dozen. I was also trained on the Gauntlet until I could emerge without a mark on me. Tanner Five said I was the only one who ever did that."

Romeo looked at Tanner Six as if he were crazy. "Dude, why didn't you just shoot the fuckers?"

"I was out of bullets, but I did have two knives. Now enough talk; it's Cody's turn."

Cody plucked the knives from the ground and stood in the center of the five poles. To do so, he had to bend one knee, hold one arm over his head, and lean backwards slightly. This was the only position in which a lipstick tip wasn't close enough to touch him.

Tanner Six shouted, "Here we go!" as he cranked the handle that controlled the pulleys.

Cody emerged at the end of the cycle with even more streaks than Romeo wore.

He looked over at Tanner Six. "This is tough."

"That it is," Tanner Six agreed. "But if you get really good at it, you'll have no fear in a knife fight."

Two weeks later, Tanner Six returned from a supply run to find Romeo and Cody working with the Gauntlet. He smiled as he rubbed a hand across his beard. Cody had practically lived inside the poles, as he was determined to best the contraption, while Romeo had improved dramatically.

Tanner Six watched as Cody ducked, sidestepped, and skipped over the flailing poles. It reminded him of a ballet he once saw. One by one, the boy knocked the lipstick tips off the poles until the ground around his feet was littered with them.

When Cody emerged from the machine after a full ten minutes, he was exhausted, sweaty… and bore only one red mark of lipstick.

Tanner Six looked at the young man who was far too close to his own age to be considered a son, and yet, nevertheless, he felt the swell of paternal pride.

"That was awesome, Cody, simply awesome."

The boy who would someday surpass his mentor shook his head in disagreement as he pointed to the lone mark on his right shoulder.

"I won't quit at this until I'm perfect. Someday I'll be the best, just like you."

Tanner Six nodded. It was all he could do, because he was too choked up to speak.

Tanner recalled his training with the Gauntlet as he found himself surrounded by over a hundred men with machetes and knives.

He had no doubt that there were firearms carried by some of the rebels, but there were none in evidence amongst the men facing him from the front of the crowd.

When the first man lunged at him, Tanner sliced a red line across the rebel's stomach with the machete and saw him retreat into the crowd.

He would kill some of these men, but that was not his main objective. The goal was to survive, and a superficial wound often served to dissuade an opponent as well as a serious injury.

Two more men came at him, one from behind, one from the left. Tanner slashed over his shoulder with the sword and impaled an eye, while the machete swung left and bit deep into a rebel's chest. He then went on the offensive, and as he brought the sword back around, he sliced open the faces of three men, even as the machete ripped apart the throat of a fourth man. The crowd of rebels reacted as one and moved back a step.

They had thought they faced a man, just an average man, but Tanner wasn't average, not when it came to killing. For more than a dozen men in the crowd that lesson would be learned at the cost of their lives.

ATOP THE HILL, SARA AND JAKE WATCHED IN AWE AS Tanner faced off against a multitude of opponents, but then broke free of their wonderment and sprang into action.

Sara's first shot hit an armed man at the rear of the crowd and sent him tumbling forward into his fellow rebels.

The sound of the shot made the entire crowd turn their heads, and down below, Tanner used the distraction to slash the sword across four throats.

Jake's first shot passed through the mouth of one man and hit the rebel behind him in the side of the head, while Sara's second shot tore apart a rebel's midsection.

The men deeper in the crowd who did have weapons pushed their way to the rear and fired up at Sara and Jake, even as Tanner continued to hack away at their machete-wielding brethren. And all the while, hot ash rained down, as the canopy overhead was consumed by fire.

FIRMAN FLED TOWARD SAFETY, AS TWO OF HIS FOLLOWERS dragged Jennifer along. As soon as he saw that the canopy that shielded them from surveillance was on fire, Firman realized they were being attacked. Then, when the white devil descended from the sky like an outcast angel, his worst fears were realized.

He wiped away a tear as he recalled the death of Gus Soe and prayed the men in the camp had sent the devil that killed the holy one to the fiery bowels of hell.

With the venerable one passed on, the mantle fell to Firman to keep the cause alive. With his lone remaining hostage, he would raise enough capital to see Gus Soe's dream come true, by trading her for an exorbitant ransom.

When they reached the ATV used to shuttle supplies from the shore, Firman ordered the men to place Jennifer inside it. Then they were on their way to the small boat that would take them to the yacht anchored farther along the coastline. The yacht had belonged to the Australian captives, and Gus Soe had confiscated it for his own use. Now, the luxury craft would be Firman's base of operations, as he took Gus Soe's place as leader, and as the ATV bumped along toward the shore, Firman daydreamed about future glories.

BACK AT THE REBEL CAMP, INSIDE THE CAGE HOLDING THE prisoners, Juan Rio let out a yelp of pain as he managed to squeeze his hips through the small hole in the corner of the cage. And as his feet sank into the accumulated urine, feces, and foul water below, he fought against the impulse to vomit.

Dr. Washburn called out encouragement to the Brit, as Juan attempted escape so he could undo the lock on the cage door.

"You're doing it, Juan, and the rebels are still distracted."

Juan held onto the rope weaved across the cage's bottom and began moving toward the edge of the pit he dangled above.

At one point, a hand slipped, and he nearly lost hold with the other, but he regained his grip by using one of the floating corpses for purchase. When he made it to the end, it took three tries to swing his legs up high enough, but soon he was lying on the ground at the side of the cage and trying to catch his breath.

"Look out!"

The cry of warning came from Melissa, and when Juan turned his head, he saw one of the rebels rushing toward him with a machete held high.

In the next instant, there came a loud crackle from overhead. Two of the corners holding the camouflage tarp aloft gave way and a huge swatch of flaming debris fell from the sky. The edge settled atop the charging rebel, while most of the debris fell on the men behind him.

Juan ignored the screams of the burning rebels and went to work freeing his friends.

AT THE SAME MOMENT THAT JUAN HAD BEEN STEPPING onto the corpse, Tanner was tackled low from behind. He fell on his back among the score of dead and mortally wounded he had created.

The men at the front of the crowd smiled and rushed forward. That's when Tanner freed the revolver from beneath the tunic he wore and shot the two closest men in the face.

That caused the crowd to surge backwards, and moments later, as the flaming debris fell, it covered most of them, while scattering the rest.

Tanner jumped to his feet amidst the confusion and chaos and followed the trail that the fleeing Firman had taken. He'd told Sara Blake that he would free her sister, and he intended to keep his word.

AFTER THE DEBRIS FELL, SARA AND JAKE RUSHED DOWN into the valley to free the prisoners, only to find that they had freed themselves. Several of the rebels had recovered their wits and were poking at the smoking debris to gather up the guns of their fallen comrades, so that they could start the fight anew, while Sara and Jake were both down to their last rounds.

A helicopter appeared overhead. Within seconds, death rained down from above as the men in the chopper fired at the rebels. The chopper soon veered off, as the wind shifted and the smoke on the ground obscured their view.

The stench of burning flesh was thick in the air. The rebels who were trapped beneath the flaming camouflage tarp were being burned alive, but their screams were fading away.

Jake fired his last round at a rebel as the man bent over to retrieve a pistol, and then Jake plucked the gun from the ground and handed it to Sara, before also grabbing up a different rifle.

After inspecting the pistol and finding it loaded, Sara passed the gun along to one of the hostages that followed behind them. Juan smiled at the weight of the weapon, although he had never held one before in his life.

Sara's final round wounded a man in the thigh, and she claimed the rifle he had pointed at her, which had only two rounds left. Afterwards, they left the camp and entered the trees, as they skirted around the fire, with Jake leading the way.

"Have you seen Tanner?" Sara said, and Jake shook his head no, while wearing a grim expression.

"All I know is that Jennifer was dragged off in this direction and there were only a handful of men around her."

The sound of the chopper seemed to come from everywhere at once and competed with the crackling sounds of the fire. After walking only fifty yards, they were free of the smoke and could make out a patch of blue in the distance.

They heard automatic gunfire and something that sounded like a muffled explosion, only to be followed by the whine of an engine. When Sara and the group with her moved a dozen more yards, they caught sight of the helicopter as it spiraled toward the water.

They ran, and seconds later, they had a full view of the beach. Sara felt her heart sink as she fell to her knees.

The chopper was partially submerged in the water. The men who had been inside it scrambled onto the shore, while farther down the coastline, a boat sped away. Sara could just make out the short blonde hair of her sister, and she wondered if she would ever see her again.

39

THE KISS OF LIFE

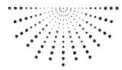

AFTER LEAVING THE CAMP, TANNER HEARD THE ATV before he saw it, and followed the sound to the beach.

He had no idea who Firman was and just thought of him as the skinny man who had been about to execute Sara's sister.

After topping a rise that led down to the beach, Tanner saw that Firman was walking toward the shore, where a skiff with an outboard motor sat just past the waterline. Behind Firman, two rebels dragged Sara's sister along, as the woman tried her best to get away.

There had been a man standing near the boat who was armed with an assault rifle of some type, possibly an AK-47. As Firman approached him, the man looked around the rebel leader, as if searching for someone. Tanner guessed that the boat belonged to the white-haired man who had died first, and that the man guarding the boat wasn't happy about anyone else using it.

The man at the boat was talking loudly and in a complaining tone, but the words were drowned out as Tanner heard a helicopter pass overhead.

When the rebels became aware of the chopper, they looked up. That's when Firman jammed a knife into the chest of the man guarding the boat. As the man fell backwards onto the wet sand, the gun he was holding fired off thirty rounds on full auto and, unfortunately for the men on the helicopter, several of the bullets had a devastating effect on the craft's tail rotor.

For just a moment, Tanner thought the helicopter had been unaffected, as the pilot soared upward to get out of range, but when the ancient Sikorsky helicopter began spiraling in an ever-tightening circle, Tanner saw that the big bird was coming down.

It landed flat but hard in the surf, and the men aboard began stumbling out into the chest-deep water. While they were doing that, Firman was getting away in the boat with Sara's sister.

Tanner took in the scene, weighed his options, and jumped into the ATV to go in pursuit. If Firman stayed close to the shoreline for just a little longer, he would still have an outside chance at saving Jennifer.

With the ATV at full throttle, Tanner sped over the sand and headed for the outcropping of rock just ahead.

WHEN JAKE POINTED OUT THE ATV TO SARA, SHE FELT her heart swell with renewed hope.

"That's Tanner!"

The two of them watched along with the hostages as Tanner kept pace and then passed the boat, as he drove parallel to it along the beach. When he reached the outcropping of rock, Tanner slowed the machine to lessen the impact. As the front wheels began ascending the craggy surface, it looked for just an instant as if the vehicle might flip backwards, as it climbed up at better than a 45-degree angle.

The vehicle reached the top of the outcropping, and after making a left turn, Tanner pushed the vehicle toward its top speed again. Just before it reached the edge that hung out over the waves, Tanner jumped up on the seat and followed the vehicle into the water.

The ATV landed forty feet in front of Firman's boat, and a skilled seaman could have easily avoided a collision. While the rebel piloting the boat did avoid colliding with the ATV, he overcompensated by turning too hard to the left. That caused the small boat to flip on its side and dump its passengers into the sea.

AFTER HITTING THE WATER, TANNER SURFACED, TOOK several deep breaths, dived, and swam toward where he'd last seen the boat. The water wasn't deep, felt warm, and it was clear enough so that when he opened his eyes, he could see.

The tunic was slowing his progress and he used precious moments to remove the garment, while mentally chastising himself for not thinking of it sooner.

Seconds later, he passed two of the rebels. One man was unconscious and floated down toward the bottom, while the second one was headed toward the surface.

Tanner unsheathed the machete and jabbed the man in the back, at the base of the spine. The man went rigid, bubbles drifted from his lips, and blood flowed from his wound.

Tanner left him, then dropped the blade to swim even faster, as a flash of blonde hair caught his eye.

It was Jennifer, kicking away frantically, with her hands

still bound behind her back. Her face was a study in panic, as the lone breath she had taken before going under was about to run out.

Tanner swam up to her, took her by the shoulders, and kissed her.

Wide blue eyes stared back at him in shock, but then she understood, and he passed along to her a portion of the air remaining in his lungs.

When the kiss ended, she nodded, and the two of them moved toward the surface, where Jennifer floated on her back and gulped in the fresh sea air.

Tanner had managed to take only one breath when he saw movement beneath the water. It was Firman. He was moving toward them with a machete gripped in his hand.

Tanner drew the revolver out from behind his back and fired it underwater without aiming, because he had no time to do otherwise. It went off while practically touching Firman's head. Firman gave Tanner one of the most peculiar looks he had ever seen, before the machete slipped from his grasp, and a line of red escaped out from a hole atop his head. Then the rebel leader drifted down toward the bottom to join his men.

After removing the small blade he kept hidden inside his bandage, Tanner used it to cut Jennifer's hands free. As they swam toward shore, she asked him a question.

"Who are you?"

"My name is Tanner."

"Tanner? Sara's Tanner?"

"Yes… I suppose."

Jennifer looked confused, but then her face crumbled, and she stopped swimming.

"Is my sister… I mean did you, did you hurt her?"

"She's the reason I'm here. We've made peace and she asked me to help save you."

"Oh, but Jake, Jake Garner, have you seen him?"

A cry came from the shore. When Jennifer followed the sound, she saw not only Sara and Jake, but also her fellow hostages. Farther along the beach, the mercenaries from the helicopter jogged toward them.

The two sisters came together in the surf and embraced tightly, while making little cooing sounds of joy. After releasing Sara, Jennifer flew into Jake's arms and the couple cried and laughed at their reunion.

Sara had been watching them with tears of relief flowing freely down her cheeks. When she turned to look for Tanner, she saw that he was seated alone on a flat portion at the base of the outcropping.

Sara walked over and settled beside him. "Thank you, Tanner. My sister is alive because of you."

"You're welcome, Blake. And this makes us even, yes?"

"No."

"No?"

"I owe you one; you went above and beyond, even for you."

Tanner pointed toward one of the mercenaries from the downed chopper.

"That man has a satellite phone. He said that transportation and medical help are on the way."

Sara stood and began walking toward her sister, but then she turned around and went back to Tanner.

"There's one more thing."

"Yes?"

Sara removed the phony wedding ring from her finger and handed it to him. "I'm leaving you."

Tanner smiled. "I knew we'd never last."

"At least we didn't kill each other."

"Not for lack of trying," Tanner said.

Sara nodded, touched him gently on the cheek, then walked away.

40

GOODBYE

Sara, Jennifer, and Jake had taken Conrad Burke up on his offer to fly home on his jet, since the plane would be landing at Bradley International Airport in Connecticut, which was just a short drive from the house owned by Sara's father.

That meant that Tanner would be flying home alone. Sara joined him outside the jet to say a final farewell.

"My sister told me about that kiss you gave her."

"It was strictly in an effort to save her, although, I will admit that I enjoyed it."

Sara grinned, and before the silence could become uncomfortable, she asked a question.

"So, what's next for you?"

"I'll see if Joe needs my help with the Russians. After that... I'm not sure, and you?"

Sara slowly shook her head. "I have no idea. I've burned my bridges with the FBI, New York City holds too many memories and, other than my time with Johnny, it feels like the last year of my life has been a waste."

"You'll think of something, Blake; you're too tough to be down for long."

They stared at each other. Neither one knowing what to say, because a simple goodbye felt somehow inadequate.

Sara stepped toward him with her hands leaving her sides. For a moment, Tanner thought she might hug him, but after stopping in midstride, she extended her right hand. Tanner reached out and shook it.

"Goodbye, Sara Blake. It's been... interesting."

Sara smiled, gave his hand a squeeze before releasing it, and then turned and walked over to Burke's jet.

Twenty minutes later, Tanner was in the air and headed back to New York City.

41
THE HOTTEST CLUB IN TOWN

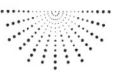

It was just after dark, and inside the Cabaret Strip Club Sophia, Laurel, Merle, and Earl all laughed along with several of Joe's street soldiers. They were watching Sammy Giacconi pantomime his version of a stripper, as he clung upside down to a pole on stage.

The act was even funnier because Sammy had loosened his long dark hair, and he flung it about in sync with the music that was playing. When he was finished, he left the stage to applause and laughter, as well as the arms of Sophia Verona.

Sophia had hugged Sammy on an impulse, but quickly released him and stepped back.

Sammy smiled. "I don't think the patrons are allowed to touch the dancers, but I won't tell if you don't."

"And who would we be telling?" Sophia said.

Sammy's smile left his lips. "I think his name is Tanner."

Sophia sighed. "Yeah, that's his name."

"Has he even called you in all the time he's been gone?"

"No."

"I would treat you better than that."

"Tanner is… different."

"So I hear, but I want you to know something, I'm not afraid of him."

"That's because you don't know him, but he'd have no reason to hurt you anyway."

Sammy waggled his eyebrows. "We should give him one."

Sophia laughed and pointed toward the bar, where Laurel sat drinking coffee. "I'm going to talk to Laurel. Why don't you work on your act while I'm gone?"

Sammy gestured at the lone one-dollar bill that Merle had tossed on stage as a gag.

"I think I'm retiring; the tips are terrible."

OUTSIDE THE CLUB, AND ACROSS THE NARROW STREET IN back, Vance lay on his stomach with a sniper rifle at the ready.

He was settled on the roof of a red brick building that was an unused warehouse. His position gave him a clear view of the club's rear exit, which was in the alley, along with a view of the small windows set high in the walls of the bathrooms.

After raising up a pair of binoculars, he saw that Fedor had also gotten into position on a roof overlooking the club's front entrance. He too was armed with a high-powered rifle with a scope.

Vance smiled.

It was time.

He made a call, and when it was answered, he said only one word.

"Go!"

Laurel was grinning as Sophia took a seat beside her. "You're weakening."

Sophia took a swig from her beer. "Tanner better get back here soon or I'm going to declare him legally dead and move on."

"You really like Sammy, don't you?"

"Too much, and he's so damn young."

"Speaking as a doctor, it's a proven fact that men are most virile at his age."

"Stop it."

"They also have amazing stamina and recuperative abilities."

"I don't like you anymore," Sophia said, and then both she and Laurel laughed.

Joe was seated behind the desk in the office when the shooting began. By the time he stood, his gun was in his hand and he went racing down the hallway.

"Laurel?"

"I'm okay, Joe," Laurel said, and Joe was pleased to see that two of his soldiers had moved in front of her to guard her.

One of the other men went to the front door and called out. "Victor? Sal?"

There was no answer, and then the man jumped backwards while looking at the base of the door.

"Gas! Gasoline."

A moment went by before a whooshing sound was heard, and the gas ignited and began to spread flames.

Joe grabbed Laurel's hand. "Everybody head to the back door in the office. Mike, you take point, and Sophia, are you armed?"

"Damn right," Sophia said, and her hand left her purse holding a gun.

The new office door was designed to close automatically and was constructed using ballistic glass that was mirrored on the hallway side. However, Joe and the others didn't have to see through it to know that the office was on fire. Intense heat was emanating from beyond the door and they could hear the crackle of flames, as smoke leaked out around the seams of the doorframe.

One of Joe's men spoke up, as he ran back toward the bar. "We can leave through the blacked-out windows up front."

The man was carrying a sawed-off shotgun. He fired it low at the glass set at the left of the doors. The glass shattered, and a gust of wind sent flames licking in at the club's interior. The man with the shotgun had his sleeve catch fire, but one of the other men quickly smothered the flames with his suit coat.

"We're trapped!" Merle said.

Joe swiveled his head around, while desperately trying to think of a way out, and wondered if for once in his life, Merle was right.

42

HELLO AND GOODBYE

Outside the club, the four young men who had killed the guards and started the fire drove off with their part in the slaughter completed. Vance stood and stared down at the club.

The building was surrounded by flames that were high enough to lick at the bathroom windowpanes. Vance felt certain that his plan had been successful and that no one would escape.

He took out his phone and called Fedor. "Is there a chance of anyone making it out of the front?"

Fedor laughed. "Not a chance. The smoke will probably kill them before the flames do."

"You're absolutely certain no one will make it out that way?"

"Da, the fire is too intense. Anyone inside that building is dead."

"That's what I wanted to hear."

Vance dropped the phone and raised up the rifle. He sighted through the night vision scope at a spot in the center of Fedor's forehead, then fired. On the other side of the club, Fedor collapsed atop the roof he was standing on, and Vance laughed to celebrate the ending of a second obstacle.

Once he was certain that Pullo was dead, Vance planned to return to Michael Krupin and execute the young leader of the Russian mob, then take his place. He was through with being Robert Vance the lackey. Soon, it would be Rurik Varanov's time to lead.

THE SMOKE INSIDE THE CLUB WAS THICKENING, AND everyone ducked down to suck in the diminishing usable air.

Merle and Earl were huddled around their sister, Laurel, as if their bodies could protect her from the growing flames. The mood among those present was moving swiftly toward panic.

When Sammy snapped his fingers, everyone but Joe jumped at the sound, but they all wondered about the smile spreading across Sammy's face.

"There's a tunnel! Uncle Joe, there's a tunnel. Granddad showed it to me years ago when he used to own the building and it was a funeral home."

"A tunnel?" Joe said, but then his eyes lit up as well. "Right. This place used to be a speakeasy back in the 1920s, but Sammy, where is it?"

Sammy ran toward the rear of the building while bent over to avoid the smoke and went down the hallway that ran alongside the kitchen.

"This way!"

There was a supply closet positioned between the bathrooms. When Sammy opened it, it was found to be filled with toilet paper, hand towels, and cleaning supplies.

The items were stacked upon a gray metal shelf, while two snow shovels, a spade for digging, and a broom were hanging from hooks on the right wall.

"There are steps under the floor here," Sammy said.

He tossed out everything he could grab and cursed when he saw that the shelving was bolted to the rear wall. He tugged at it and the metal only creaked.

One of Joe's bodyguards moved beside Sammy. "We got this, kid. Bosco, give me a hand."

Sammy stepped out and one of the other big men squeezed into the small space beside his friend. They ripped the shelving away from the wall with ease.

Once they had stepped back outside with the rack of shelves, Sammy got down on his knees in the doorway. He reached in and pulled up a piece of stained and dirty carpet to reveal a wooden door set in the floorboards, with a recessed brass ring as a handle. The club was filling with acrid black smoke. When Sammy pulled up on the door and released the musty air from below, it smelled sweet compared to the air above it.

"Where does it go?" Laurel asked, and Sammy answered her.

"It goes under the street and up inside that old warehouse over there. But listen, it's just wide enough to walk single file and the other side is covered over with a hardwood floor, we'll have to break through."

Joe grabbed the metal spade from off its hook and handed it to the largest of his men.

"Big Ralphie, once we get over there use this on the wood, and everybody turn on your phones, we'll use them as flashlights."

Big Ralphie went down the narrow stone steps first, then Joe took Laurel by the hand and helped her to step down, next went Sophia, and then Joe, followed by the rest of them.

Earl was the last man into the tunnel. He reached up and brought the door down to keep out the smoke, which had grown so thick that only three feet of space separated it from the floor.

The tunnel was surprisingly deep, about a hundred feet long, smelled of dirt, and was littered with debris from its crumbling brick walls and ceiling.

The narrowness of the passage engendered claustrophobic feelings and Big Ralphie's wide shoulders became wedged in twice before he made it to the other side and started up the second set of moss-covered stone steps.

Laurel began to walk up the steps, but Joe reached past Sophia and held her back.

"Big Ralphie's going to need some room to swing that spade."

He was right, as the huge man stood hunched over six steps from the top and repeatedly swung the tip of the shovel at the wood blocking their exit.

It took over a dozen good whacks before a hole appeared between two boards, and six more before the gap widened a few inches. That was when the wooden handle of the spade broke and rendered it useless.

Big Ralphie appeared to Joe as if he were about to cry, as he took in the broken tool, but then anger lit his round face. After practically lying down atop the steps, Big Ralphie managed to turn himself around until he was facing the others. After climbing up the steps backwards and hunched over, he pressed his wide back against the floorboards and strained to stand up. The big man's face looked scarlet in the light from Laurel's phone, as he pushed with all he had. When the wood broke, it was like the shattering of a window, and Big Ralphie stood triumphant, with his smiling face above floor level.

They had emerged into a basement. Less than a minute later, everyone had scrambled up a flight of wooden stairs and into the vacant warehouse, where they were grinning at each other in relief.

A metal gate could be viewed through the glass of the front door, making that exit unfeasible. Everyone stared across the street at the flaming building they had just escaped from and realized how lucky they were to be alive.

Joe led everyone to the rear, and with one mighty kick, Big Ralphie opened a small door. The group piled out into the trash-strewn parking lot under the light of a full moon.

Joe smiled at Sammy. "Way to go, kid. We'd be toast if not for you."

Sophia spun Sammy around, leaned against him, and raised her head to kiss him. "My hero."

Sammy took her in his arms, but the kiss lasted just a second, as everyone looked up at the man standing halfway down the metal fire escape. The man was laughing, had a long rifle slung over his back, and was pointing an AR-15 at them.

"Vance," Pullo spat out.

Vance pointed at them. "Everyone take out the guns nice and slow and place them at your feet."

The men complied, and as they did so, Sophia eased her hand inside her purse.

Vance clucked his tongue at her. "Sophia Verona, it's so nice to finally meet you. Now drop the purse or I'll blow your head off."

Sophia let go of the purse and it hit the ground between her and Sammy just as a shot went off. For an instant, Sophia thought her gun had somehow fired from its impact with the pavement. That thought fled from her mind as Vance let out a cry of pain, bent over in agony, and tumbled off the fire escape.

That's when the figure in black appeared. He was holding a gun at arm's length and walked over to stand above Vance. Vance stared up at the man who'd shot him and knew he was about to die.

"Hello, Vance. I was wondering who fired that shot from the rooftop."

"Tanner? But I heard you were—"

"Goodbye, Vance."

The shot that followed was nearly drowned out by the blaring sounds coming from two arriving fire trucks. Tanner holstered his gun as he walked over to join the group, noticed the sparkle of Laurel's engagement ring, and then looked at Sophia, who was still in Sammy's arms.

He sighed. "Whenever I go on vacation everything changes."

Sophia went to him, and as they kissed, Sammy hung his head.

"Tanner?"

"Yeah, Joe?"

"Are you ready to get back to work, buddy?"

Tanner gazed over at Vance's corpse.

"I've already started."

TANNER RETURNS!

TWO FOR THE KILL - BOOK 8

AFTERWORD

Thank you,

REMINGTON KANE

JOIN MY INNER CIRCLE

You'll receive FREE books, such as,

SLAY BELLS – A TANNER NOVEL – BOOK 0

TAKEN! ALPHABET SERIES – 26 ORIGINAL TAKEN! TALES

BLUE STEELE - KARMA

Also – Exclusive short stories featuring TANNER, along with other books.

TO BECOME AN INNER CIRCLE MEMBER, GO TO:
 http://remingtonkane.com/mailing-list/

ALSO BY REMINGTON KANE

The TANNER Series in order

INEVITABLE I - A Tanner Novel - Book 1

KILL IN PLAIN SIGHT - A Tanner Novel - Book 2

MAKING A KILLING ON WALL STREET - A Tanner Novel - Book 3

THE FIRST ONE TO DIE LOSES - A Tanner Novel - Book 4

THE LIFE & DEATH OF CODY PARKER - A Tanner Novel - Book 5

WAR - A Tanner Novel- A Tanner Novel - Book 6

SUICIDE OR DEATH - A Tanner Novel - Book 7

TWO FOR THE KILL - A Tanner Novel - Book 8

BALLET OF DEATH - A Tanner Novel - Book 9

MORE DANGEROUS THAN MAN - A Tanner Novel - Book 10

TANNER TIMES TWO - A Tanner Novel - Book 11

OCCUPATION: DEATH - A Tanner Novel - Book 12

HELL FOR HIRE - A Tanner Novel - Book 13

A HOME TO DIE FOR - A Tanner Novel - Book 14

FIRE WITH FIRE - A Tanner Novel - Book 15

TO KILL A KILLER - A Tanner Novel - Book 16

WHITE HELL – A Tanner Novel - Book 17

MANHATTAN HIT MAN – A Tanner Novel - Book 18

ONE HUNDRED YEARS OF TANNER – A Tanner Novel -

Book 19

REVELATIONS - A Tanner Novel - Book 20

THE SPY GAME - A Tanner Novel - Book 21

A VICTIM OF CIRCUMSTANCE - A Tanner Novel - Book 22

A MAN OF RESPECT - A Tanner Novel - Book 23

THE MAN, THE MYTH - A Tanner Novel - Book 24

ALL-OUT WAR - A Tanner Novel - Book 25

THE REAL DEAL - A Tanner Novel - Book 26

WAR ZONE - A Tanner Novel - Book 27

ULTIMATE ASSASSIN - A Tanner Novel - Book 28

KNIGHT TIME - A Tanner Novel - Book 29

PROTECTOR - A Tanner Novel - Book 30

BULLETS BEFORE BREAKFAST - A Tanner Novel - Book 31

VENGEANCE - A Tanner Novel - Book 32

TARGET: TANNER - A Tanner Novel - Book 33

BLACK SHEEP - A Tanner Novel - Book 34

FLESH AND BLOOD - A Tanner Novel - Book 35

NEVER SEE IT COMING - A Tanner Novel - Book 36

MISSING - A Tanner Novel - Book 37

CONTENDER - A Tanner Novel - Book 38

TO SERVE AND PROTECT - A Tanner Novel - Book 39

STALKING HORSE - A Tanner Novel - Book 40

THE EVIL OF TWO LESSERS - A Tanner Novel - Book 41

SINS OF THE FATHER AND MOTHER - A Tanner Novel - Book 42

SOULLESS - A Tanner Novel - Book 43

The Young Guns Series in order

YOUNG GUNS

YOUNG GUNS 2 - SMOKE & MIRRORS

YOUNG GUNS 3 - BEYOND LIMITS

YOUNG GUNS 4 - RYKER'S RAIDERS

YOUNG GUNS 5 - ULTIMATE TRAINING

YOUNG GUNS 6 - CONTRACT TO KILL

YOUNG GUNS 7 - FIRST LOVE

YOUNG GUNS 8 - THE END OF THE BEGINNING

A Tanner Series in order

TANNER: YEAR ONE

TANNER: YEAR TWO

TANNER: YEAR THREE

TANNER: YEAR FOUR

TANNER: YEAR FIVE

The TAKEN! Series in order

TAKEN! - LOVE CONQUERS ALL - Book 1

TAKEN! - SECRETS & LIES - Book 2

TAKEN! - STALKER - Book 3

TAKEN! - BREAKOUT! - Book 4

TAKEN! - THE THIRTY-NINE - Book 5

TAKEN! - KIDNAPPING THE DEVIL - Book 6

TAKEN! - HIT SQUAD - Book 7

TAKEN! - MASQUERADE - Book 8

TAKEN! - SERIOUS BUSINESS - Book 9

TAKEN! - THE COUPLE THAT SLAYS TOGETHER - Book 10

TAKEN! - PUT ASUNDER - Book 11

TAKEN! - LIKE BOND, ONLY BETTER - Book 12

TAKEN! - MEDIEVAL - Book 13

TAKEN! - RISEN! - Book 14

TAKEN! - VACATION - Book 15

TAKEN! - MICHAEL - Book 16

TAKEN! - BEDEVILED - Book 17

TAKEN! - INTENTIONAL ACTS OF VIOLENCE - Book 18

TAKEN! - THE KING OF KILLERS – Book 19

TAKEN! - NO MORE MR. NICE GUY - Book 20 & the Series Finale

The MR. WHITE Series

PAST IMPERFECT - MR. WHITE - Book 1

HUNTED - MR. WHITE - Book 2

The BLUE STEELE Series in order

BLUE STEELE - BOUNTY HUNTER- Book 1

BLUE STEELE - BROKEN- Book 2

BLUE STEELE - VENGEANCE- Book 3

BLUE STEELE - THAT WHICH DOESN'T KILL ME- Book 4

BLUE STEELE - ON THE HUNT- Book 5

BLUE STEELE - PAST SINS - Book 6

BLUE STEELE - DADDY'S GIRL - Book 7 & the Series Finale

The CALIBER DETECTIVE AGENCY Series in order

CALIBER DETECTIVE AGENCY - GENERATIONS- Book 1

CALIBER DETECTIVE AGENCY - TEMPTATION- Book 2

CALIBER DETECTIVE AGENCY - A RANSOM PAID IN BLOOD- Book 3

CALIBER DETECTIVE AGENCY - MISSING- Book 4

CALIBER DETECTIVE AGENCY - DECEPTION- Book 5

CALIBER DETECTIVE AGENCY - CRUCIBLE- Book 6

CALIBER DETECTIVE AGENCY – LEGENDARY – Book 7

CALIBER DETECTIVE AGENCY – WE ARE GATHERED HERE TODAY - Book 8

CALIBER DETECTIVE AGENCY - MEANS, MOTIVE, and OPPORTUNITY - Book 9 & the Series Finale

THE TAKEN!/TANNER Series in order

THE CONTRACT: KILL JESSICA WHITE - Taken!/Tanner - Book 1

UNFINISHED BUSINESS – Taken!/Tanner – Book 2

THE ABDUCTION OF THOMAS LAWSON - Taken!/Tanner – Book 3

PREDATOR - Taken!/Tanner - Book 4

DETECTIVE PIERCE Series in order

MONSTERS - A Detective Pierce Novel - Book 1

DEMONS - A Detective Pierce Novel - Book 2

ANGELS - A Detective Pierce Novel - Book 3

THE OCEAN BEACH ISLAND Series in order

THE MANY AND THE ONE - Book 1
SINS & SECOND CHANES - Book 2
DRY ADULTERY, WET AMBITION - Book 3
OF TONGUE AND PEN - Book 4
ALL GOOD THINGS… - Book 5
LITTLE WHITE SINS - Book 6
THE LIGHT OF DARKNESS - Book 7
STERN ISLAND - Book 8 & the Series Finale

THE REVENGE Series in order

JOHNNY REVENGE - The Revenge Series - Book 1
THE APPOINTMENT KILLER - The Revenge Series - Book 2
AN I FOR AN I - The Revenge Series - Book 3

ALSO

THE EFFECT: Reality is changing!
THE FIX-IT MAN: A Tale of True Love and Revenge
DOUBLE OR NOTHING
PARKER & KNIGHT
REDEMPTION: Someone's taken her
DESOLATION LAKE
TIME TRAVEL TALES & OTHER SHORT STORIES

SUICIDE OR DEATH
Copyright © REMINGTON KANE, 2015
YEAR ZERO PUBLISHING

This book is a work of fiction. Names, characters, places and incidents either are products of the author's imagination or are used fictitiously.

Any resemblance to actual events or locales or persons, living or dead, is entirely coincidental.

All rights reserved. Except as permitted under the U.S. Copyright Act of 1976, no part of this publication may be reproduced, distributed or transmitted in any form or by any means, or stored in a database or retrieval system, without the prior written permission of the publisher.

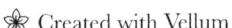 Created with Vellum

Printed in Great Britain
by Amazon